My Dearest Husband:-

My Dearest Husband:-

Elizabeth Riggs

Writers Club Press
San Jose New York Lincoln Shanghai

My Dearest Husband:-

Writers Club Press
an imprint of iUniverse, Inc.

For information address:
iUniverse, Inc.
5220 S. 16th St., Suite 200
Lincoln, NE 68512
www.iuniverse.com

ISBN: 0-595-24252-9

Printed in the United States of America

This book is dedicated to the descendants of
Celicia Elizabeth Riggs Ingels.

Contents

Foreward

When I read my grandmother's collection of letters, I knew they should become a book. I decided to allow the letters to speak for themselves but added fictional narration, based on family stories and knowledge of Lizzie's personality, to enable others to understand the circumstances under which the letters were written. Following the story of the letters from August 1893 through February 1894 in *My Dearest Husband:*– I have appended edited writings from Lizzie's 1885 journal, an essay she wrote at Gallia Academy, and the letters which Berte wrote to her during their courtship before the 1890 marriage. Together, these pieces provide a window through which we can view Victorian times and life on the Ohio River.

1

Leave-taking

Heat waves shimmered across the graveled lane. August had poured humid air into the basin of the Ohio Valley again this year of 1893. Wearing her customary black ankle-length skirt and spotless white shirtwaist with the fashionable leg of mutton sleeves, Lizzie Ingels marched from the house to the buggy carrying her two-year-old son Clair. The wilting petticoats clung to her legs. Perspiration rolled down her back, the short wisps of hair curled damply on her forehead, and Clair's little arms around her neck felt like hot flannel, yet her heart was chilled. She did not want to say "Good-bye" again.

Her husband, Berton Ingels, carrying the cracked black leather valise once more, followed Lizzie from the farmhouse. Larger pieces of baggage had already been stowed in the buggy as well as a paper-wrapped parcel of bread, hard-boiled eggs, and cheese for the journey.

"It won't be so bad, Lizzie. I'll have my appointment before you know it, and then you and Clair will be joining me in Nebraska before it gets cold." Berte caught Lizzie's hand and walked beside her. "It will be wonderful starting a new life for the Lord in a new land. As the preacher's wife, you'll be such a helpmate. I love you so, and I'll miss you, but we have to remember this is our calling. We have to be patient." He placed his hands on Lizzie's shoulders, looked into her blue eyes and admonished, "Read your Bible every day and pray for me to succeed in my calling. I'll write you whenever I can, and your letters will help keep me from getting homesick." Then Bert Ingels put his arms around his wife and drew her towards him, folding Clair into a family hug.

Tears glittered in her eyes, but they didn't spill. Her voice, strained and soft, Lizzie replied, "Oh, Berte. I don't know how I can do this by myself. It will be so hard selling off our furniture and animals and packing for our trip West. I can't hardly believe I can do it alone. Thank God I have Clair to keep me company, but I will be missing you so." Lizzie paused, blew her nose, and continued, "It's only been three months since you came home from your term in Delaware, and that was such a long winter without you. Pray for strength for me, Berte. I will need it sorely."

She moved out from under his arms and stood back. Clair wriggled in her arms so she deposited the little boy in the lane but kept his hand in hers lest he run too close to the horse's hoofs. Lizzie swallowed hard and continued, "Now, I've packed you enough food for several meals on the train so you don't need to spend money for any, at least till Chicago. Then, do remember to be frugal. You should be able to find simple sandwiches that don't cost too much. Desserts will be much too costly. We have to stretch every penny, you know." Then her voice wavered, and she quickly brushed away the tear that escaped, despite her will to be strong.

Berte, unable to speak as well, came to her and wrapped her in his arms. He kissed Lizzie gently, squeezed her shoulders, and then swung away into the buggy where Mr. Morris, their neighbor, waited to drive him to town. Lizzie watched through misty eyes as her tall, handsome husband climbed up. Even in this heat, her Berte wore a waistcoat and jacket. His old shirt looked pretty good since she had turned the collar. Today, his shoes were freshly polished, as well. She had seen to that last night. His hair was neatly trimmed, and his mustache made him look distinguished. He certainly looked like the preacher he was intent on becoming.

Raising his hat, Berte tilted it towards his wife and son, and then placed it on his head, adjusting it to just the right angle. Sitting erect and dignified, Berte waved once more as the buggy started off towards Gallipolis where he would catch the train to Chicago and from there to

Omaha and on to Farnum in southwestern Nebraska. His eyes, as he turned toward the road ahead, were bright with anticipation. Despite Clair's attempts to pull her back to the house, Lizzie stood watching until the buggy disappeared from the horizon. Then she bent to pick up Clair, buried her face in the little boy's neck, and blindly headed for the porch.

2

Hopes and Plans

Hands shaking, Lizzie Riggs carefully opened the envelope. She clutched it to her bosom with one hand and led Clair with the other to her favorite chair in the sitting room, the oak platform rocker that had been a wedding gift. She always felt closer to Berte sitting there. With Clair wiggling in her lap, Lizzie found it impossible to concentrate as she would like on Berte's letter. So she gave him a quick hug, kissed his cheek, and dismissed him, "Clair, you go play with your ball now. I want to read Papa's letter from Nebraska." Lizzie sat with careful posture, her feet tucked neatly beneath the black bombazine skirt. Her shirtwaist collar, fastened snugly at her neck, would stay in place with the polished brass collar pin securely holding it. One of her tiny hands repetitively touched her cropped hair as she smiled at the contents of the letter. The careful center part could not corral the bangs symmetrically. One curl, defiant as its owner, rebelled. Steel-blue eyes, known to have pierced a body through when necessary, softened as she read Berte's words. She felt giddy as Berte's carefree younger sisters. It was good to hear from her husband at last.

After reading the letter, Lizzie called her son from his play and carried him upstairs for a nap. He wouldn't lie down until his mother promised to nap with him. The bedroom was warm, and a bottle fly buzzed under the lace curtain, but a little breeze stirred the air enough that Clair was soon asleep. Lizzie eased herself off the bed, relishing the chance to answer Berte's letter undisturbed. She had chores to finish, but they would wait today. She was surprised at how blue Berte seemed in his letter. Lizzie had thought he would be so busy that homesickness wouldn't bother him. She smiled a little at this reaffirmation of his love for her. Questions bubbled forth as she contemplated all that had to be done before she could join him. There were so many questions, but the mails were agonizingly slow. It would be a long wait for her husband's advice. She had best hurry to get her questions down on paper and away with the next mail.

Angola, Ohio
August13, 1893

Dear Husband:--

What do you ask for the three plows, and what shall I do with those harrow teeth? There hasn't been anyone here to buy any yet, only one man who came to see the wagon. Mr. Vincent sold the same kind of wagon last week for $37.50. Did you mean it would cost $1.75 per hundred things packed in boxes? Grandma Lattin only had to pay $1 from Florida. I am going to ship my fruit anyway if it does cost me something for we have so much of it, and we will want it so bad this winter.

I can sell all three of the tables and one bed and the stove. Several have come after things already, and they are good pay, too. I sewed some pieces of old straps together yesterday and made a right good pair of lines for the buggy.

I wrote a card to Joe Newton about those knives you gave him to sell. I told him we would give him half of the profit of any he sold. If he can't sell them, I will go myself so as to get shed of them as soon as possible. I will write to Joe to either bring the knives he has to your mother's or the money for them. Who were the parties you left those other knives with out back of Bladensburg? I am going to try and collect enough to pay your brother Jap and Mr. Blackburn what we owe for the knives.

Don Burns has been sick with the fever, and there is very little hope. I have been nearly down sick since you left. For two days I had the flux real bad but am better now.

As I told you, you would leave me with the hardest part to do. Ma and Pa feel awful bad about us going and hurt because you didn't ask about going or say something more about it. I have tried my best to smooth things over, and if you get a good place, it will help to get them reconciled to my going out there. I will have things ready here so I can start there in two days after you send word where to ship to.

Everyone here says I will not go for you will come back. If you ever intend to do anything I want you to do your <u>very best</u> for the next six weeks, for your work now will decide whether you get a good place this fall. You must trust the Lord to aid you in your preparation of talks. Spend lots of time on your studies and visit among your people. You must learn to be friendly with every one. I never did feel so anxious for you to do well as I do now. I feel that if you are ever going to preach at all, it must be right now at the beginning of your ministry.

When I received your letter today, I was surprised at your state of feeling. I pray the Lord has made your way brighter, and you have received the necessary light that you needed so much. I felt awful blue and discouraged a little while about your going, but now there is peace, and I feel that is what the Lord wants us to do. I have worried about you having to stay so long in Chicago and then having to pay your way from Holdredge on to Farnam. I was afraid you would not have enough money to carry you all the way, but I just put the care of that on the Lord to open up the way for you in some way.

I shall never ask you to come back here unless we all get real sick. In some way we can make enough to live on. I want you to be as saving as you can with your money for it is such hard times now. No one has any money scarcely.

We are both well but it is real warm here today. Lots of love and may the Lord send you a wonderful blessing is the earnest prayer of

Your loving wife,

Lizzie

Lizzie sealed the envelope and sat thinking. It was exciting to anticipate moving west. Her entire life had been spent here along the Ohio except for that one journey to New Orleans after her graduation from Gallia Academy eight years ago. That next fall she had worked on the boat as cook and laundress when her uncle and brothers had taken their produce down the Ohio to the Mississippi to sell in New Orleans. But that had scarcely been a pleasure trip where she could enjoy sights along the way. She wanted desperately to see more of the world. She could hardly imagine a city like Chicago or crossing the Mississippi River to Missouri. Traveling with Clair alone across the country would be difficult, but she was confident she could do it. A new life with Berte as a successful Methodist pastor's wife sounded so good. Her family and their friends had been simply hateful about her husband. They didn't understand him.

Teaching in their little school just wasn't right for him. He had thought that was what he wanted to do and had studied for a time at Normal School in Lebanon before their marriage. But, after spending a few years teaching, the Lord had called him. Berte had told her about that day on the hill when the Lord had spoken to him clearly, and Berte knew that he wanted to serve Him from then on. He had known for a year what he was expected to do; yet he shrank from the responsibility of preaching.

Berte had instead been tempted by the stability of the farm and persuaded himself that he had not truly been called to preach. But that day on the hill, Berte could avoid it no longer. That experience had led him to Delaware, to Ohio Wesleyan University, for a semester of classes to prepare him for the ministry. They were separated then, too. The 150 miles might just as well have been the thousand that kept them apart this time. It had been hard. Without little Clair, she would have been unable to stand it. Ma and Pa were more than disappointed that Berte had not been satisfied either with teaching or with farming the land they had given the newly-weds for a wedding present. Now they wouldn't believe he could stay committed to his calling. Their comments on his fickleness regarding career choices hurt and angered her.

Berte would surely find a position in the Nebraska conference soon. Certainly the letters from Nebraska had assured him that there would be work available in that state. She was anxious to join Berte and help him in his work for the Lord. Six or seven weeks—then she and Clair could travel west, too. Smiling, she rose from the little desk and headed for the kitchen. It was time to get dinner ready for the boarders. Callie, the hired girl, would just have to do the potatoes tonight. Lizzie would concentrate on the ham and the string beans. Perhaps a berry cobbler for dessert? If only Callie has finished her picking this morning, instead of complaining about the heat and the chiggers, there should be enough black raspberries. Lizzie sighed and stepped quickly down the narrow back stairs to her kitchen to fire up the cookstove.

3

Exasperation

"Callie. Callie! Calleeeee Sue!" the voice from the kitchen cried, exasperation rising at the failed response. Callie, out in the yard under the black walnut tree, appeared not to hear. Her shoes were off as she nibbled at one of the early apples. The crisp fall day with sky so blue demanded appreciating, and that's apparently just what Callie aimed to do. Lizzie could holler all she wanted. Callie remained planted under her tree. The long white apron was stained with the morning's apple-butter making, and she seemed too tired to care what her employer wanted from her next. Callie's long braid swung lazily as she leaned back, appearing to contemplate God's gift of the day.

The back screen door squeaked and then slammed shut as Lizzie strode onto the porch. Carrying Clair in one arm, she peered left and then right while she shielded her eyes from the bright sun. Squinting, she, at last, observed a slight motion on the other side of the big tree.

"Callie," she called in an exasperated tone. Clair chose that moment to squirm through his mama's arms to the floor. Lizzie watched him from the corner of her eye but kept calling to the hired girl, "I need you right now in the kitchen. I've already put the beef roast and the carrots and parsnips in the oven, but you must get the potatoes peeled and boiled ready for mashing. I've been waiting a long spell for you to come help me in the kitchen. Now, most of the supper work is done—except for the potatoes and some biscuits. You can start the biscuits after the potatoes are set to cooking." As Callie meandered toward the porch door, Lizzie stooped to pick up her son who had wandered out to the yard heading for a bite of apple from Callie. "I have to take

Clair upstairs and change him. I declare, if and when I ever get him trained, I'll be the happiest woman alive." Lizzie continued talking even as she headed upstairs with the baby, "I started setting the table, but you can finish it when the biscuits are baking."

She sighed as she changed the little boy's diaper cloth and remembered her recent letter to Berte. She had told him then in no uncertain terms that if Callie didn't start behaving better towards her and getting her work done on time, then she would have to get a new girl. A few days later, she had got up the gumption to give Callie a piece of her mind. Lizzie had had a struggle even getting Callie to wake up that morning to start the breakfast. Then, Callie had told Lizzie she had no intention of sleeping downstairs this winter. That was the last straw. Lizzie always slept on the first floor in cold weather because the downstairs bedroom stayed warmer. This winter, with Berte away, she wanted Callie to be near. She had told Callie that if she wouldn't stay downstairs, Lizzie would just quit housekeeping and let her neighbors take care of her. Afterwards, Lizzie had felt proud that she spoke her piece, and Callie, if sullenly, had stayed down with her since then. However, every day seemed to have its new ordeal with her hired girl. Just the other day, Callie had been drying out Lizzie's pretty washbasin, the white with blue flowers that she dearly loved. Not paying attention, Callie let it slip from her hands, and the bowl crashed to the floor. Now she had to use the graceful pitcher with an odd mismatched basin. If only Berte were here, Callie wouldn't be so outrageous. It felt like she had two children to take care of when here she was paying Callie to help her.

Later, at the supper table, Clair sat in his high chair demanding more milk. He drummed his little spoon on his tray and squealed because his mother was serving the boarders. Mr. Callahan complained that the butter dish was empty; Mr. Butler wanted more potatoes; the Rev. Morgan's wife seemed disappointed that the cobbler was apple rather than her favorite cherry. Lizzie felt as though she could satisfy no one. Besides, she had been counting on raspberry cobbler herself. Callie, as her employer had feared, had given up too soon on the berrying.

As Lizzie rushed to pour Clair's milk, the first stabs of a headache began behind her eyes. She was familiar enough with the beginning signs; these headaches had plagued her since she was in high school at Gallia Academy. The doctor then had tried all the powders and syrups he had. He had even insisted she cut her hair to the cropped bob Lizzie still wore. Nothing had helped. The only thing that had changed was that Lizzie was now far too busy to retire to her room in the dark solitude that might bring some relief. Instead, dishes needed washing, and the floor required sweeping, and firewood called to be stacked. When, at last, Lizzie laid her head on her pillow, she wished only for a full night's sleep. Clair had wakened her twice the night before. Counting the throbs in her temples, Lizzie remembered she had not written to Berte today. Ah, she thought, I'll probably be awake before dawn again. I'll write then. With that thought, the blessed sleep came.

4

Mistress of the Farm

Weary from shucking corn all morning, Lizzie climbed on to the wagon seat and coaxed Prince towards her father's farm, a mile south of hers. Queen Anne's Lace and bright cornflower chicory lined the road, and Lizzie smiled in greeting those, her favorite wildflowers. As she crossed Raccoon Creek, a gentle rain began and dimpled the dark water. The shower soon stopped. Suddenly, Lizzie reigned in Prince and stared in fascination at the panorama before her. A vertical column of variegated ribbons formed in the sky. Clouds prevented the formation of the complete rainbow momentarily, and the view to her seemed to be an unfinished painting. As she sat watching, the clouds rolled away, and the column transformed itself into a full rainbow and then, as a miracle, into a double rainbow. Awed, Lizzie murmured, "My goodness, what a painting that would be!" Her mood brightened as she enjoyed the miracles of nature around her.

After a while, she flicked the reins and urged the horse forward. Shortly, she approached the fine brick house, which her grandfather, James Riggs had built, perched high on the ridge above the flood plain. The big "R" on the front proudly signaled the family name to all who passed. At the Riggs farm, her father's hired hands unloaded the thirty-three barrels of big potatoes and sixteen of seed potatoes. Her father came down to the wagon to oversee the unloading. "Good morning, Daughter. I sent word we would come for the potatoes. You needn't have brought them down."

"I know, Pa, but you've done me a favor by buying them from me. It was my job to deliver them to you."

"That's my girl!" her father smiled. Jacob Riggs had told his daughter that her ability to handle the farm business made him proud. He had acknowledged that it had not been easy with Berte away, but that Lizzie showed good sense in running her farm. In fact, he said, she showed good sense in every thing but her determination to join his son-in-law in Nebraska. He had made it very clear that her intention to join Berte was impractical and impossible. Lizzie needed to stay safe here with her family, he had told her over and over. Today, however, he didn't pursue the familiar lecture. Instead he listened to her accounting of recent sales.

"I still have four barrels left for my own use this winter and a barrel of hog potatoes, Pa," Lizzie continued. "I sold one pig for $1.50 to Mr. Lawson; Ella wants two for $1.00 each, and Callie will take one for $1.00. I know you were able to sell some for $1.25, but I am just grateful to get rid of these before it gets cold. I plan to sell the big hog and buy a smaller one for my own use this winter. Times are so tough. With the panic about silver in the country, no one seems hardly to have any cash." She gave her father a quick hug and smiled. "I surely wouldn't without your generosity, Papa. Thank you for the $10.00 loan you gave me. That means I can pay off all our debts. I will go without things before I will ever go in debt for even 5 cents again. I thought debts weren't so bad, but now I think they are terrible and so hard to pay them off. I'm planning to sell some knitting so I can pay you back as soon as possible."

Her father chuckled. "Well, my girl, I see you're learning about money the hard way. You're right about the lack of cash around here. Hardly anyone has two nickels to rub together. I'm right proud of you working like a man down there on your farm. I just wish to Heaven that your husband was by your side. He should be!" The rising volume and clouds across his face signaled a storm approaching.

"Pa, please," Lizzie pleaded. "Don't start in again about Berte." She turned abruptly, anxious to stop her father's comments and climbed again into the wagon. Jacob Riggs offered his arm for support and helped her up, but his expression was dour.

"Well, he should be here with you this winter! There now, I won't say any more. Are you warm enough? Don't let Prince get carried away. Keep him under control. Sometimes he just wants to run ahead. Be sure he knows you're the boss, Lizzie."

"Yes, Pa. I'm fine, and I'll drive carefully. Come down home and see Clair. He's growing like a little weed. Tell Ma 'Hello'. I've got to get back and do the laundry while the sun's out. I'm out there in the wash-house more than in my home. There are so many sheets and towels to redd up for the boarders. Seems like my work's never finished." Lizzie waved, grasped the reins, and guided Prince down the drive. Behind her, her father shook his head as he watched her progress down the hill towards the river road.

◆   ◆   ◆

Prince trotted smartly. As Lizzie turned into the lane to her house, she wondered again at the blessings of the Lord. He had given, through her parents, this prime piece of farmland to her and Berte. Together they had built the two-story white frame house, not alone, of course, but each had had a part in the actual construction. Like the men, she had driven nails, solid and sure. She was proud of her home now.

From the road along the river, anyone could admire the solid character of their home. Unpretentious but sturdy, reflecting their personalities, it stood watch as the big Ohio flowed by. From its front porch, a visitor could enjoy the steamers filled with travelers or the keel boats loaded with produce gliding so near. Conversations carried across the water, and when a neighbor passed by, a friendly "Halloo!" sounded. The real road was the river. It was dependable. All you had to do was run up the flag at Riggs' Landing, and you could be off to Gallipolis or Marietta upriver or downriver to Huntington, Cincinnati, or even New Orleans. The dirt lane, which she had just driven with Prince, was far less reliable. If it rained a solid soaker, the road was impassable. Winter ice made it dangerous. Summer sun dried the ruts into unyielding obstacles. But the river had always been her love, and she felt privileged to own property that skirted it. It transported her produce to far away markets; it soothed her; it fascinated her; it carried her on its currents. A playground in winter for skating, a place to dangle your feet on a hot summer day, entertainment from the dish boats which stopped to sell their wares. Lizzie loved "La Belle Riviere." It would always be a part of her.

The interior of the house showed Lizzie's labor and love at every corner. Lacy curtains, stitched by her, draped the long, stately windows. Braided rugs graced the bedroom floors, and flower-filled appliquéd quilts invited the weary to rest. On one wall hung the oil of white poppies that she had painted on black tin, framed in ornate gold leaf. That was her favorite painting, but then she had always loved flowers. She had even created a scrapbook of flowers, an herbarium, that had earned her honors for her senior biology project. Next to the window, a mountain scene of a little white church, reminiscent of her Clay Chapel, gave hint of her desire to see other landscapes. Clay Chapel certainly was not nestled in a mountain scene like this was. No matter, whenever she passed either the painting or the little church of her childhood, Lizzie was reminded of her faith. The largest of her paintings, also completed before her marriage, was a hunting scene, but Lizzie had never liked it so it was somewhat hidden behind a door. Lizzie thought it was a cruel picture and wondered why she had ever chosen to spend so much time on a subject she didn't like. Her nimble fingers had dressed and decorated her home, but other necessary projects always called. Someday, she hoped, she would again have the luxury of enough time to paint, unlikely as it seemed in these busy, busy days.

Lizzie had woven her spirit into her house and her land. Both welcomed her now. It wouldn't be easy to leave her home in the care of others, but she yearned to see her husband and the world. She had to know what the rest of the country was like. Then, maybe she could come home to Ohio and be content.

But now, that laundry called. She still had enough time to rub the sheets, wring them out and peg them on the line to dry now that the sun was out. At least there was time if Callie had begun heating the water out in the washhouse. Tomorrow, being Tuesday, she would iron the sheets with her flat irons and set Callie to washing up the clothes although she hated not getting all the wash done on Monday. It always threw off the rhythm of the week when the wash wasn't finished on Monday. She didn't vary her schedule very often. Let Callie's hands get a little rough and red like hers, she thought, as she rubbed her own hands and frowned.

5

Reign of Terror

Lizzie sat near the quilting frame stitching. She never just "sat" in the parlor to chat as her guests and some members of her family did. If she wasn't hemming a dress or darning socks, she was braiding a rug or, as now, quilting. Under her nimble fingers, the pastel prints of her "Flower Garden" became three-dimensional, taking on new life. These flowers inside the house would brighten her bedroom as much as her hollyhocks and petunias brightened the yard outside. She had been working for over a month on this quilt and by now the stitching was almost automatic so she could listen and take part in the conversation around her as she pieced the quilt blocks in tiny even stitches. She could see well enough by lamplight for this task, but when she got the quilt in the frame, she would need daylight to do the quilting.

Berte's little sisters, Lida and Sallie, had come for a visit. Their chatter often annoyed Lizzie. She wearied of the constant prattle about clothes and young men. They seemed so young to her although, of course, she was only eight years older than Lida. With her responsibilities as a wife and mother alone, their silliness irritated her more than the needle stabs to her finger. Tonight, however, Lida happened to mention an incident from the past. "Mr. Morris told us today that a long time ago there was a boat on the river that brought death to Gallia County," she said.

Lizzie's mind ceased its wandering, and she responded to the girls. "A long time ago, I declare!" she fumed. "Not so long ago I can't remember. Do you want to hear about it?" At the girls' affirmative nods, she began to tell the story.

"I was about 14 when the *John Porter* came upriver that summer, right about my birthday time, from New Orleans. I think it was about 1878, and I know it was in August. We heard about its passage long before it appeared. Yellow Fever had struck several crew members, and they were put off at Vicksburg. However, more and more of the crew got sick, and many died.

"As they came upriver, all the towns and landings were scared. Nobody wanted them to tie up. No one wanted to let them into their communities. People threatened the crew, and their supplies dwindled. They weren't given new supplies. Seventeen crew members died in all.

"You can imagine how we felt as we waited for that boat to continue upstream. I happened to be out front on the swing when I saw the *Porter* go by. It was really strange. There was no sound at all coming from the boat—no sounds of the crew working and certainly no greetings either from the boat or the land. It was like a ghost boat sliding through the water. I felt all shivery and ran towards the house, but Pa and Ma had come outside, too. We stood, all quiet, as the boat passed by.

"When the boat tied up at Gallipolis, they quarantined her. A committee of townspeople visited her and helped give supplies, but she was told to get out of the city as soon as possible. At first the crew had trouble getting past where that boat had sunk near the island, and then they needed to do some repairs on broken down equipment. In the meantime, several more died. The crew was so down hearted they swore they simply couldn't go on. The current carried the boat back downstream near Clipper Mills where they managed to anchor. Now you know how close Clipper Mills is to us here! We were very frightened to have that boat of death so close to us.

"But it stayed and stayed. A watchman guarded the boat. No one was allowed off. Only the doctors were allowed to board. That boat became a curiosity to the river folk. I can remember on sunny days, a whole parade of buggies would drive slowly by the river road. We drove by several times, and I was just scared to death. Ma made us hold our handkerchiefs over our noses just to be safe. I just held my breath until we were up the road.

"Finally, they disinfected the boat. When everyone thought it was safe and the danger was past, a lot of people from the county went on board to see the boat just out of curiosity. And then, there really was panic. Thirty-five of our people died after being on or even near the boat where it anchored. Many others were sick for a long time. Not just men—women, too. You know the Howards? Well, the grandmother was one of those poor souls who would never again see the light of day. I was so glad Papa wouldn't allow us to step foot on that boat! Ouch!" Lizzie squealed as the needle pricked her finger. "Gracious! I've bled on my quilt." Deftly, she spit on a clean finger and rubbed at the spot. It soon disappeared, and Lizzie continued with her story.

"The town just about shut down. Businesses closed for about six weeks. The streets were just empty. They burned coal tar fires on the street corners to try to keep out the disease and fumigated everyone who had been near that boat. The boat tied up about six weeks altogether. It was very frightening to everybody. Yellow Fever came calling, and nobody wanted her here.

"I don't remember just how it happened, but in the fall, the river rose some, and the barges from the boat floated away. I guess the doctors who were on board disinfecting were able to tie up the *Porter* again to save her. Some of the barges were rescued, but several were lost. They burned one because it had so much disease it couldn't be disinfected, and some scared river men burned some others. At last, though, they were finally able to hire a new crew for the boat, and it disappeared from our waters and headed south for home.

"I still can't go by that spot on the road where the cliffs come down so close to the water without seeing that ghost boat in my mind. I shiver every time we go past. No, I don't think Gallia Countians will forget that terrible time anyway soon," Lizzie punctuated the end of her story by jabbing her needle into the quilt.

The girls had been silent during the telling of Lizzie's story. It was rare for her to speak so long. It was rarer for them to be still so long. The next time they passed through Clipper Mills, perhaps they, too, would imagine the *John Porter* tied up too near the shore and feel goose bumps crawl up their spines.

"That's enough stitching for tonight. My poor fingers are sore. Who wants some popcorn?" Lizzie asked, then smiled as her two charges practically fell off their chairs in a rush towards the kitchen. Poor Berte, she thought. He'd be missing his beloved popcorn. She hoped he was as homesick for her as she was for him.

6

Disappointment

Forgetting her dignity and feeling like a girl again, Lizzie fairly skipped back across the lane from the little store and post office,. After several fruitless days, her reward had finally appeared. Now she clutched her letter from Berte, and her feet flew back to her house where she would, hopefully, find out about the job Berte had surely taken by now so that she could join him. Anxious as she was to read the letter, she, nevertheless, took time to carefully slit the envelope with her letter opener. Like the others, she would refold this precious letter and return it properly to the envelope for safekeeping in her little wooden box. Then she could take it out and savor it again and again. The house was quiet in the early afternoon, and Lizzie settled in her rocker to read.

September 12, 1893

Dear Wife:--

I will write you today as I haven't much to do right now but to study. I intend to devote the rest of my time to study. I promise you that I won't go to school very long, but I would like to go to Denver and take Elocution and Oratory. As far as money is concerned, it would be better for me to go to school. I know I could get work now as the Conference is bound to get me some when I pass my exams, but I will not be able to get much at all in the way of salary in the kind of work I can get now. If something wonderful is offered, I will take it, but if not, I will go to Denver and rent rooms, and you can come. If you would rather not, you can remain there awhile longer if you can stand it. It's mighty hard on me without you, but I believe I can stand it a while longer.

I am satisfied now that I can make a success. I am gaining confidence right along. I now know just what I need to brush up. As far as money matters are concerned, I know we will not suffer.

Well, love to you and Baby. I can't hardly stand it if I think of you and Baby. Good bye.

Aff. your Husband,

B. H. Ingels

I think I will get about $30 from this place. At least that is what is due from the people and the missionary money. But, as it is such hard times, I am afraid they won't pay right now. I haven't any money and don't know where I will get enough to go to Conference unless you sell something right away and send it to me. It will cost me about $3.00 for the round trip.

Lizzie sat stunned. She couldn't believe what she had just read. Not take a job? Go back to school? She to stay here alone without Berte? Her hands trembled; she shivered despite the warmth of the room. Silently, Lizzie turned the envelope over and over in her hands until she realized it was not empty. Another folded letter fell out as she turned it upside down. Had he changed his mind? She read eagerly:

Sep 13, 1893

Dear Wife:--

I am so glad that I came out here. I have received more light from the Gospel of Jesus Christ since I have been here than in all my life. If I do not receive any money at all, I will be well paid for having come. I am perfectly assured that I have found my work. I have joy and delight in it. I know now why the old Pioneer Minister could rejoice and be happy and get $00.00 salary. I am happy not at times only but almost continually. I hope, not only *hope but know, that you will be made happier in your labors as assistant pastor.*

I do want one year in Theological School so I shall be better prepared to enter a more responsible place and not lose any money in the long run either. I can make more in one year then than I can here in three now. I am anxious to be successful in the start of my career. My little experience here has shown me just what I need, a better voice with a little more confidence.

I am just as sure of success now (if I keep my health at all) as I am that I am living. I know that the Spirit is the power but how are we to use it to be the most effectual without considerable training? The soldier doesn't know how to fight or to use the sword until he has been trained to it. I wish you could be reconciled to my going to school. I consider your judgment as being very good, but it does seem to me now the best plan now is to do as I have told you. Now I am willing to let you stay with your folks awhile, if you wish. When we get so lonely, we can't stand it any longer, why you could pull up and come out. I will not insist on your coming against your will. Now I would not insist on having my own way in this matter if it wouldn't add to your happiness more than my own. If I wasn't sure of success, I wouldn't insist on having my own way because I wouldn't feel like spending money for naught, but I can succeed. Good-bye. Love to you and Baby.

Aff. Your Husband,

B. H. Ingels

In an abrupt move, Lizzie stood up and wiped her eyes. She stomped towards the little wooden box and shoved the envelope inside. "How dare he?" she thought. "How can he ask so much of me? How can he be so gloriously happy in his work without me beside him? I want to go, too! I really want to go." She stamped her foot. The black, laced boot thumped satisfactorily on the pine floor. Then Lizzie wilted and slumped to the floor, nose running, tears pouring. After a few minutes, Lizzie reached up to her box and withdrew the letters. Reading them through again, her tears rained down. The letters lay in her lap, tear-splotched, as she sobbed, resting her head on the tapestried cushion of the rocker.

At length, she heard a door close. Gathering herself to an upright position, Lizzie smoothed her hair, wiped her eyes with her apron hem, and blew her nose on the lace-edged handkerchief always ready in her sleeve. Carefully, she refolded the letters and placed them in the box; this time dark stains blotched the words. Straightening her shoulders, she went to greet the hired girl.

Late that night, sitting at the little desk with her flannel nightgown tucked around her feet, Lizzie wrote fast without pause. She poured out her thoughts and feelings to her husband so far away—farther away than ever tonight.

October 1, 1893

Dear Berte:-

Until last night I have never given up the idea that you would take that excellent offer of $75 per month and not go to school, but today I got your letter. I think you have gone against the best chance you ever had, and that was not called for this year! <u>Christ may have called you to preach, but he never called you to go to school this year and leave your family in the way you have.</u> I have met with many disappointments, but I never have had one that was as hard to bear as this one. It seems to me some times that I cannot bear it at all.

It has not only disappointed me but so many others as well. Mrs. Morris has gone so far as to move most of her fruit over here and had made arrangements to move in here this week. Pa was to have gone with me as far as Chicago, and now that will have to go along with the rest of the disappointments. And now I won't be able to go anywhere this entire winter for I am ashamed to meet anyone. I will not move from here until you take work if that is never!

Your own father even said you have done wrong in not taking that work. He thinks you should wait until next year to go to school if you still want to.

I have only 9 cents and no prospects for getting any more. I have knitted 37 skeins of yarn this year and have only been able to get a few nickels for all that work. I cannot sell Prince. Brother Ed took him and was gone for three or four days last week trying to sell him, but no one wants to buy now. Everything in the house would have been gone already, but I keep telling everyone that I don't want to sell things until I am ready to break up house-keeping. Now, to think I will have to stay here all this long lonely winter is more than I can stand. I will not go home to stay for then Clair is even harder to care for, and now he worries the life out of me even here at the house he knows.

You told me in your letter not to scold, but I cannot help it when I feel what a mistake you have made. The loneliness of the situation grieves me. It is different with you. When you are lonely in the house, you can go out doors and away. I am tied here hand and foot and can't get away. Berte, if you love us at all and want us to come to you, please, oh please, take that work if it ain't too late. You do not realize what you are doing when you refuse to take that place. You let your desires for school overbalance your respon-sibilities to your family.

Pearl and Burt were here today to tell me good-bye. I was ashamed to face them and wouldn't tell them good-bye for I will have to stay here until spring. By that time, you will say you guess you will not stay out there and be back here again. Then I can go through with the same thing again in a few months. If you ever want us to come to you, you must get work and stick to it. You keep changing your mind every day, and you are depending on your father for money. He hasn't any. He had to borrow money to pay his taxes, and it is too hard to get now. No one that has money wants to lend it now, for times are too hard. That money I got from Jim, I promised to pay back in a month. Not one cent has he had from us and no prospects to get any for him either. He needs the money now, too.

You must not write to me for any money any more for I haven't any nor can I get any. I will have to pay what we owe with what I do get, and that is very little. If you want to go to school, you will have to earn your own money. It is all I can do to keep Clair and myself. If you had failed in your examinations and hadn't any place offered, then I would have done any-thing to have helped you gain more schooling. But now, when you have refused $75 and could have saved enough to go back to school in a year, I can't work hard enough to make any to send to you. I have sent you $10 since you have been away and gave you $50 when you left. I can't help you any more.

My Dearest Husband:-

Please let me know what your final decision is immediately. If I stay here, I must get my coal and things fixed for winter.

Your wife,

Lizzie

I am just broken hearted now. Jim Crafts was taken down with the fever yesterday.

7

Certainty

While Lizzie fretted about the uncertainty of her winter plans, she was quite aware of the certainty of death. Lizzie had watched Death come, within her family and within her community, not only to the aged but also to apparently strong, healthy young folks as well as many new-born babies. The fever, consumption, childbirth, diphtheria, whooping cough—all those words caused terror in Lizzie. As soon as she got word that Ella Westover was sick, she had written to Berte. She had, of course, done all she could to help Ella and her husband and young baby. She had carried pies and roasts and warm breads, hoping to tempt Ella's appetite. When she returned home this fall day, she had to accept that Ella would soon follow Death's beckoning hand. Through tears, she wrote:

October 11, 1893

My Dear Husband:-

It is with a sad heart I try to write. Poor Ella Westover may never see the dawn of day again on earth. I just left there and there is very little hope of her living until morning. She has had bilious fever, and now it has gone to her brain. I was there most of the afternoon yesterday, and she talked the whole time when she was conscious. Both doctors were there yesterday, and they said there would be a change by this morning. All have given her up. She had said she must get well for her family. Poor Joe. It is almost killing him. They thought all the time she was getting better, but she just kept getting worse. I will go down later to see how she is.

I received your card last night. If I thought we could meet most of our expenses out there, I would come right away. I feel now that I can't stay here all winter alone. Pearl will take the big plow for $5. Prince worries me the most. There just doesn't seem to be any way I can sell him. I want to come so bad now; I don't see how I can wait much longer. I am so sorry now I didn't make up my mind to go this week as I intended. Pa went to St. Louis, and I would have gone that way instead of by Chicago so I could have had company. I haven't said anything to the folks up home about going and am almost afraid to for fear they will not want me to go.

Ed has gone east to buy apples. The new preacher came yesterday. There are seven children. I think that is too many children for any preacher to have.

Jim Crafts have a little boy at their house. She is real poorly I guess. Well, I must close and see to getting Callie up to get breakfast. She doesn't want to get up early.

Aff. from

Wife Lizzie

Two days later, Lizzie updated Berte about their friend Ella.

Angola, Ohio
October 15, 1893

My Dear Husband:-

I have been to Sunday school and church and have come home to get something to eat and rest a little. Then I will go down to see if Ella is living. She was resting easier this morning.

She got so happy yesterday morning and talked to everyone of her folks. I never heard anyone talk as nice as she did yesterday. She told them she was going to die and told Joe not to go to any expense to bury her because it didn't matter. She said we are clothed in the robe of righteousness. She talked to Uncle Dock and told him she wanted him to meet her in Heaven, that Jesus would take him to himself if he would only give himself up. She wanted us to tell all Epworth Leaguer and Sunday School Scholars to give their hearts to Jesus now before it is too late. I never heard anyone talk so nice, nor would I have missed hearing her for a great deal. Joe said he wouldn't take a fortune for her talk yesterday morning.

I think that it is worthwhile to try to live a Christian life and even suffer so when we die, we can die as happy as she was. She said she could see into Heaven and Oh what a grand and glorious place it was. One glimpse of it was enough to make everyone want to give their hearts to Jesus. I think her sickness will be a great blessing to many a one.

Pearl said you had written to her for money. I was in hopes you was making enough to pay all your expenses, but if you are not, I don't see that it will do for me to go out there. Berte, I cannot go out there and work hard enough to meet the expenses for both of us to stay there. And, I cannot stay here and be exposed to the rain and storms the way I have been. I cannot stand it. By spring, they will have to lay me beside the other girls up there in the graveyard. Write me just as soon as you get this letter and let me know how long you intend to go to school. Then I will know how to plan my work. Callie has been cranky again, and I think it impossible for me to put up with her all winter. We will have to get another girl unless you decide to work soon. Clair is feeling better, but he gives me so much more trouble now that I feel I can't stand under the burden much longer.

Aff. Your Wife

Lizzie

Ella died about three or four o'clock this morning.

    Ella's proclamation of her faith and her vision of Heaven awed Lizzie. If only she could work with Berte as co-pastor! There was so much to do and so few willing to do it. Lizzie decided she would try to do what she could and be contented, but she would be happy in spending every moment in working for Jesus. Ella's funeral prompted her to share it with Berte through another note.

Angola, Ohio
October 18, 1893

My Dear Husband:-

Ella Westover was buried today at 12 o'clock. She looked real natural. They lined the grave with muslins and ferns and flowers on it. All that saw it thought it was nice and pretty. The flowers on the casket were beautiful. I didn't go to the grave because I stayed down at the house and took care of the baby for them. It was right good today but cried some. It has been sick ever since Friday when it took cold. It is such a sweet little thing, and if we were going to live here, I would be almost tempted to tell Joe I would take it. He will break up housekeeping, but I don't know what he will do yet. I didn't ask because he feels so bad I couldn't bear to bother him. They had sent to Huntington for a Baptist preacher.

Ma and Pa are so opposed to my going to you now until you get work. They say so much moving at this time of the year will be too hard on me. But I feel I can't stand to stay here any longer without you. If you had taken work, they wouldn't have said a word against my going, but as it is…I will go up home today and see if I can't get them to give their consent (providing you can get a house free of rent.)

Your aff. wife,   Lizzie

8

Denial

"**S**on, promise Mama you'll be very good at your grandmother's today. It's really important to Mama that you be quiet while I talk to Grandma and Grandad. I need you to be my good son," Lizzie spoke with an urgency her son had not heard before.

"I be good, Mama. I your good boy. I love you," the little boy cooed as he scooted closer to his mother on the seat.

The ride down the river road seemed endless today although it was only a little more than a mile. Lizzie couldn't help watching the river as they drove. Its peace couldn't calm her nerves today although she usually found solace in its quiet beauty. Even though the late October sun warmed the air, and the maples along Raccoon Creek burned crimson and gold, Lizzie did not respond to her favorite season of the year. She didn't even notice the sumacs that flamed along the road behind a display of purple asters. As they turned to go up the hill to her parents' home, Clair solemnly promised again, "I'll be so good, Mama." She switched the reins to her left hand and hugged her son close to her.

"Thank you, dear. I know you'll help Mama today," she murmured as she took back the reins in both hands to make the turn to the hitching post.

Jack, her father's hired hand, ran from the barn to help Miss Lizzie from the buggy. He swung Clair down and then turned his attention to Prince. Lizzie sighed. Having someone take care of her for a change was a treat.

Mama and Papa came to the door, stepped out, and met her on the path to the house. They seemed delighted with a visit from their daughter and their spirited grandson. Though they lived so close, it was rare to have visiting time since Lizzie was always busy at her own house. As they hugged, Lizzie tried to control her shaking hands. Elizabeth Guthrie Riggs looked inquiringly into her daughter's blue eyes. Lizzie hoped Mama wouldn't notice the tiredness and pallor she had seen in her own mirror this morning.

"Well, Lizzie," her father said. "This is a surprise. How did you manage to get some time for a visit when you've been so busy with your boarders lately?"

"Callie promised she would get dinner ready tonight. I really need to talk to you both today," she fidgeted and looked down, not meeting her father's eyes.

"Well, of course, Lizzie. Anytime. You know that. What's on your mind?" he inquired. The older man took his daughter by the arm and led her to her favorite chair in the family area of the dining room.

His kindness was almost too much for Lizzie. After this week's hard work and worries over money and homesickness for Berte, she trembled at the softness in his voice. It was good to be home. It was good to know she was loved. "Oh, Papa and Mama! I miss Berte so much. It has been so hard all this fall without him here. I have so much responsibility on my own. I want to be with my husband. I want to take Clair to his father. I want us to be a family again," she burst into terrible sobs, which she had vowed she wouldn't do.

Jacob Riggs looked at his wife above his glasses. Worry wreathed his face. He stroked his beard with one hand and awkwardly patted Lizzie's shoulder with the other. It was obvious to see that he hated to see his little girl so overcome. He paced with his hands held tightly behind his back while his wife moved to comfort Lizzie. Clair came to stand beside his mother and looked puzzled into her face, softly touching her cheek.

"Does this mean you have heard from Berte that he has taken a position in Nebraska? Has he found out what kind of salary he will get?"

Jacob paused. When no answer came from Lizzie, his voice grew louder. "Does your silence mean, 'No', my girl? Answer me, please."

"Oh, Papa, Berte feels that he must take more classes before he's ready to preach. He is so happy that he has found his field, but he feels he needs more training to do a better job. He wants to take classes at the University in Denver. So, no, he hasn't taken work yet." Lizzie had stopped her wild sobs and gained back her composure although she was sniffling and dabbing her eyes.

"In God's name," her father's outburst made clear his feeling, "how does he expect to support a family then?"

Her mother joined in, although in a quieter tone, "You know you aren't well enough to work long hours to bring in money while Bert's at school. I don't understand how he can even ask you to come to him."

"Oh, Mama. I want to go to him. I am so lonely without him. I am working hard here every day. I can work there, too," Lizzie pleaded.

Jacob smashed one fist into his other open hand. "I just cannot understand, for the life of me, why that man had to leave here in the first place. I know he thinks he has a calling, but he has a wife and a child. He has a perfectly good living right here on this river bottom on the land we gave you. Why wasn't he content to settle down and farm?" he stormed as he circled the room.

Clair's eyes widened at the outburst from his grandfather, and he scrambled up to the safety of his mother's lap. She scooped him up and held on to her little one for comfort as she faced her parents. Clair's head was buried in her neck. "Papa, I am surprised at your reaction. You have such a strong faith in God. You always support our minister and Clay Chapel. Why are you surprised that Berte has found a calling that is not to the land. His family has always been devoted to the ministry. You know his family has produced circuit riders, and Alexander Church was named for Berte's ancestor, Alexander Waddell. Don't you think Berte can succeed as a preacher of God, too?" Lizzie dropped her head to plant a reassuring kiss on the top of Clair's head.

"Now, now," her mother patted Lizzie's hand and cleared her throat, "we have to remember Bert doesn't always finish what he begins. He went off to Normal School over at Lebanon and was all set to teach. How long did that last? Then, you built your house on your acreage, and he intended to farm it. Instead, he left you to go to Delaware to learn about the ministry." Elizabeth dropped her hand and took a step backward. "Now he's out west asking you to give up your home and run to him. You must see how we feel. You're our daughter. You're frail. You cannot handle this move by yourself. And you certainly can't handle a move that will find you in a strange land in the dead of winter with no money to support you."

Her father continued his wife's recital. "Your mother's right, Lizzie. We want you and Clair to stay right here where you are safe and secure. There's no way we can let you take off to your husband until he has work to support you. Who knows if he will even stay out there? Given his record, he could be back here before you even get to Colorado. We can't give you our blessing for that long, uncertain trip. You know we are right!"

"What I know is I love my husband! I know I want to be with him!" Lizzie shouted, pulled Clair to her bosom, and raced out of the room with him clinging to her, down the path, and to the buggy. Her face twisted, but the tears did not come as she lifted Clair up and then followed herself. Her quick motions caused her feet to tangle in her long skirt. There was a tearing sound as her heel caught the fabric. She reached down, extricated her foot, and grabbed the reins. Glancing back, she saw her parents on the porch. Mama's hand was raised to her mouth. Papa stretched his arm towards the buggy imploringly. But, Lizzie raised her whip and startled Prince who raced quickly down the hill towards home. Clair stared at the silent woman beside him who was suddenly a stranger. Her mouth was set; teeth were clenched. The little boy scooted away from his mother and found comfort in his thumb. For once, his mama didn't notice and pull it away.

That night, while Clair slept, she wrote a succinct postal card to Berte.

Angola Ohio Oct 21 1893

My Dear Husband:--

I am so sorry but Pa and Ma will not give their consent for me to go west until you take work. They say as soon as you take work I can go but not until then. I am almost killed at the way they talked about it. I suppose I deserved it. It is too hard. I will try and be as patient as I can but it is awful hard.

In haste, Aff. Lizzie

Turning out the oil lamp, Lizzie crawled wearily into bed. Sleep would not come, and the weight of heartbreak seemed to crush her. There were no tears, but her eyes stared vacantly into the dark room. She turned over and reached for Berte's solace, forgetting. Then, a torrent of tears soaked her pillow. It would be a miserable winter alone without her Berte.

9

Envy

So, Berte was homesick. Well, good, Lizzie thought. That serves him right! Today the mail brought her word of the adventures her husband was having without her, and Lizzie was jealous. Berte had found a little house that he thought they could have for $2.00 or even less if they papered the walls. Two dollars might as well be one hundred as far as she was concerned. Why couldn't Berte understand there just was no money. And here he was talking again like she could just drop everything and catch the train to be with him because he was lonely. Well, let him try to take care of boarders and a small boy and a reluctant employee. See how long he could stick it out in her place. Not long, she guessed.

Then, he had had the nerve to expound on the wonders of the land where he was. It was the "greatest place in the world for outdoor exercise" and "anyone who works at it improves in health right along." Exercise! She guessed she got enough exercise running up and down the stairs and bending to scrub the floors and lifting heavy baskets of wet sheets and towels to hang outside whether the wind was blustery and cold or it was stifling hot. It must be nice to have enough time to deliberately exercise outdoors yet. But in her mind's eye, she could see Berte, tall and straight, with his hat tilted ever so slightly, striding down a country road with the great Rocky Mountains as a backdrop. What a picture that would be. She wished with all her heart she could see it in real life.

His letter continued with instructions for finding her way to University Park, four miles from Denver. He seemed to expect her in Colorado immediately. She just didn't understand how that would ever happen yet Berte apparently saw no obstacle to her joining him right away. Where did he get his optimism? That boy needed to learn the realities of life, she fumed.

But Lizzie had chuckled when she read about the lesson her errant husband had learned in his absence. Berte had written:

I am awaking up to the fact that it doesn't pay to be unmannerly and distant and selfish. I have always taken pride in appearing thoughtless of good manners, but here I have observed how unpleasant it is to be in company with a man of that sort and how pleasant it is to be with a man whose manners and politeness comes from the heart. It is not always put on and just too formal as I used to think. I guess that is why I tried to appear eccentric. There is no advantage to being eccentric. I think I am improving in that line as well as in some others, yet there is still great room for improvement.

Many times she had scolded Berte for his lapses of etiquette, especially his habit of eating his favorite peach pie or coconut cake before his meal—so that he wouldn't be too full to enjoy it. Indeed! Perhaps being out in the world was good for him after all.

Oh, but it just wasn't fair. He had seen something Lizzie would have given her eyeteeth for. Berte witnessed firsthand the Republicans celebrating their Grand Jubilee in Denver. Everyone there had rejoiced that Ohio had gone Republican. Anytime Ohio was mentioned, the 6,000 people in the Coliseum would create a tremendous applause. That must have been something. To be so far away from home and hear your own state honored like that. How proud Berte must have been! If only she could have seen that, too.

At least Berte valued her opinion. She knew she was lucky to have a husband who recognized she had her own thoughts and was willing to listen to them. Berte was not like most of the men she knew. Her husband, unlike so many others, wasn't afraid to give women their due. She recalled his telling about hearing Susan B. Anthony's speech in

Delaware last spring. He had been impressed by her ideas. Of course, he had to amend his thoughts by adding "for a woman." But, now he had asked for Lizzie's opinion on the text for his next sermon. She knew the text, John 14:12, "Verily, verily, I say unto you, he that believeth on me the works that I do shall he do also and greater works than these shall he do because I go unto my Father." She only hoped she wouldn't be too tired tonight so that she could study her Bible. Berte wanted to hear her ideas. That was something, anyway. They would be a team in the ministry someday soon, she hoped.

10

Adventure Awry

The November breeze blew chilly, but the sun shone warm as Lizzie and her sister Rose climbed into the buggy. Prince pawed the ground impatiently, his nostrils smoking, as the young women settled on the bench, pulling afghans over their knees against the cold. This rare opportunity to be alone, taking care of this morning's chores in Gallipolis, counted as an adventure for them. When Lizzie drove to her parents' home to pick up Rose who still lived in the family home, she left Clair in his grandmother's care.

Taking the reins and holding them tightly to curb Prince's exuberance, Lizzie watched as Rose climbed up and carefully adjusted her skirts. Prince was certainly frisky today. Lizzie sighed. How she missed having Berte there to drive and help up the ladies. Instead she had had to scramble up herself, surrendering all dignity, and be responsible for keeping Prince under control. Well, nothing was going to spoil this day of freedom for her.

Lizzie felt as if she were released from prison for the day. "It is wonderful to get away from the house for awhile," Lizzie remarked. "Sometimes I feel like I am tied to that place and all of my responsibilities. I brought ham sandwiches and apples for our lunch. Then perhaps we can have some ice cream for dessert at the Park Central. That would be such a treat for me! Orange-pineapple, I think. That's my very favorite." As the horse trotted towards Gallipolis, Lizzie's cheeks pinked in response to the freedom as well as the cool air. Lizzie recited her errands, "I need to pick up a few supplies from the Wholesale Grocers on Court Street, and if we have time, I'd really like to stop by the milliner's to see if she has a pretty but inexpensive feather to replace the one that's molting on my hat."

"Oh, Sister, it is wonderful to have the day with you alone," Rose replied. "When Clair is with us, much as I love him, there's precious little time for us to talk. He's so active and so curious that he always keeps both of us hopping just to stay one step ahead of him. Maybe today we can get all talked out."

"Really, Rose, do you really think that's ever possible," Lizzie laughed. I surely wish we could see each other more often. I miss talking to someone who listens as well as you do—or my Berte. Callie and Clair don't seem to be very good substitutes in that department."

The buggy passed Clay Chapel set high on the west side of the road. Their grandfather had given the land for the church; their parents continued their support; the family lives were intertwined with the little Methodist chapel. It was just north of the family home. Walking through the grape arbor from the house, one would emerge into the cemetery on the hillside where rested most of their departed relatives, the Guthries and the Riggses. The simple white clapboard building with its modest steeple dominated the landscape as it looked down on the rich river bottomlands farmed by their father. As always, both young women glanced towards the chapel from the road.

"Are you planning to go to the Class Leaders' Convention next week, Lizzie? Pa, Uncle Jim, and Amos Clark will all be taking part, you know."

"I certainly hope I can go up for part of it anyway. It's such an honor for our own little Clay Chapel to hold an important meeting like that. I heard one of the topics to be discussed is 'Is the Class Meeting Essential to Methodism.' My goodness! I'd say it certainly is. I only wish Berte could be here for this meeting. He'd have so much to offer and be able to show off his preaching abilities to all those visitors. Remember when Berte and I went up to the camp meeting right after our wedding? It made a right nice wedding trip. He made me proud the way he could lead discussions and give such beautiful prayers.

"By the way, did you see the advertisement in the *Tribune* for wool flannel at Halliday's. It's only 50 cents a yard. I wish I had an extra $3. I could make Clair and me winter cloaks in matching shades for our Colorado trip. Well, I guess we'll have to make do with our old ones if Clair can still wear his," Lizzie paused mid-conversation as she pulled on the reins slightly to slow Prince.

"If I could, I'd buy it for you, Sister. It's just nobody has any spare cash these days," Rose frowned as she spoke. "I spent all my savings foolishly on that marble-topped dresser. Oh, but I do love it, Lizzie. The mirror is so pretty, and the little glove drawers are just plain fun. Don't you love the carvings on it?"

"Now you know I'd never let you spend money on us," scolded Lizzie. "And I, for one, am glad you bought your dresser. It's about time you did something nice for yourself. You deserve that dresser.

"My, doesn't the river look pretty today," Lizzie continued. "I really love this view down the curve of the river. It sometimes seems as if half my soul is river. I remember what wonderful times I've had traveling on the Ohio. That summer when I graduated from the Academy, I had my biggest trips. Remember when Grandma Riggs took me by boat all the way up to Matamoras? I got to meet so many of our cousins and had such a pleasant time. I had never known that it was our ancestor, James Riggs, who came down the river in a flat boat and founded Matamoras, but when I met half the town named Riggs, I certainly learned about the family history.

"By the way, did you always know about Jack Powers? I had never heard the story of how they put Grandpa James and Jack, who were both babies, in saddlebags over the horse when Bazel and Mary Riggs left Maryland to come across the mountains and join Bazel's father near Matamoras. Bazel and his wife brought a few slaves with them, and the story is that their Ohio neighbors were upset at their owning slaves so that's why Bazel's family moved to Virginia, across the river at Ravens Rock. When he grew up, Grandpa moved on here to Gallia County, and Jack moved there, later on, to work for him. Jack was a free man by then, and he moved in to that little house on the farm where he still lives.

"Anyway, what with all the visitors calling to see us all along the way up the river, it was really exciting even if I did get rather homesick. I never knew we had so many cousins!"

Rose didn't answer. She had heard all of this before, more than once, and nodded appropriately although her mind was elsewhere. She stifled a yawn politely. Lizzie, released from her prison and having an adult to listen to her, kept chatting.

As Lizzie was speaking, Rose realized the horse's tempo had quickened. Her hands instinctively tightened on the edge of the buggy. Lizzie, not aware, continued, "Then, that same fall I got to go to New Orleans when Pa let me go on the boat down river to sell the summer produce. It was hard work cooking and doing all that laundry for the men, but I did get to see a little of the world that summer. Now I just want a chance to see a different part of our country. Those Rocky Mountains must be beautiful and so different from here."

"Speaking of the Rockies," said Rose, relaxing her grip on the buggy as Prince seemed to settle down, "what do you hear from Berte these days."

Lizzie appeared to be cheerful as she related Berte's experiences in Colorado—how he had been present at the Republican Jubilee and how well his studies were going. As she chatted on, a little too brightly, Rose watched her intently. Lizzie was concentrating on how to phrase her words. Rose mustn't know how she really felt about Berte's wonderful life so far away from her.

"Say," interrupted Rose, quickly changing the subject, "Did you read in the paper about that baby they're raising in an incubator box? Just like baby chickens! He's lived 13 days now in what they call his 'summer resort.' Isn't that a miracle? Rose suddenly gasped and then yelled, "Oh my, Lizzie! Hold tight to those reins!" The buggy swerved wildly.

"I'm trying to. Whoa, Prince. Whoa! My hands aren't strong enough!" Lizzie screamed back.

The buggy lurched as Prince broke from his trot and galloped down the hill to Chickamauagua Creek at the edge of town. The buggy rattled behind the horse, throwing its passengers from one side to the other. An afghan fell out. Rose scooted towards Lizzie on the seat and tried to grab the reins from her. Lizzie didn't relinquish them but allowed Rose to hang on. Her heart pounded as loudly as Prince's hooves. The added pressure to the reins made no difference to Prince. He ran even faster. As they thundered towards the livery, a man sprinted into the street, caught the bridle, and succeeded in stopping the horse and its buggy. The sudden stop threw both women to the floor. Lizzie's eyes were wide, and her mouth made little o's, but no sound came. She prayed they wouldn't fall out and under the horse's hooves.

"Dear God…Help us!" she cried, grabbing for the bench post to stop her from sliding out of the buggy.

The liveryman, Paul King, had succeeded in stopping Prince even though he was tossed aside by the frightened horse. Now he turned his attention to the driver and her passenger. Rose scrambled down the step, re-positioned her hat, and smoothed down her disordered petticoats and skirt. But Lizzie climbed painfully back on to the bench where she sat dazed. Paul had to lift her from the buggy. As they stood near it, the nervous horse kicked out. One kick struck Lizzie's left leg, and she crumpled to the ground. Rose also received a kick, but she remained standing. She bent to rub the spot. Paul gently carried Lizzie to a box so she could rest while they assessed the situation. The apprentice was dispatched to fetch the doctor from his office on Fourth Street.

When the doctor arrived, Lizzie finally allowed the tears to come. Her leg pained her greatly. A deep scratch on her face trickled blood; she hurt from head to toe. Tomorrow all those sore spots would turn to purple. Moreover, Lizzie was mortified when she realized her limb was in plain sight of the men in the livery although they took great care not to stare. That added to her anguish. Not only did her body hurt, but also her pride. Lizzie had always been smug about her ability to handle horses. What had gone wrong?

"There now, Mrs. Ingels, you're going to be all right. I've put salve on the leg wound to help it heal and bandaged it for you. It might be fractured so I don't want you to put any weight on it. You'll have to use crutches for some time, I'm afraid," Doctor Howard said as he replaced bandages and bottles in his bag.

Too upset to answer, Lizzie let Rose take charge. Rose announced, "I think we will need to stay in town tonight. Mr. King, can you take care of Prince and hitch another horse to our buggy? A gentle nag will do just fine. We don't much want to deal with Prince again today. I'll drive us over to our aunt's. Someone will get word to our parents from there. Thank you all for your help today. Mr. King, I reckon if you hadn't stopped that horse, he'd have run us clear into the river. We owe you a great deal." Paul King, still shaky from the near catastrophe, led Prince to a stall and tethered him carefully. Then, he led a tame older horse to the buggy and secured the reins for the ladies. As the doctor and Paul lifted Lizzie into the buggy again, Rose made sure the skirts stayed in a respectable position.

Sitting straight and tall on the bench seat, Rose carefully turned the horse towards the city square. Ordinarily, the sight of the pretty park located above the river where the first French settlers of the city had built their log cabins, thrilled both her and Lizzie. Today, they scarcely noticed it nor the pretty bandstand in the middle of the green expanse that honored the veterans of the Civil War from Gallia County. The buggy crawled down the main street and passed the hotel with its broken promise of the orange-pineapple treat. The women ignored the shops and businesses that had promised entertainment for the day. Instead, they traveled two more blocks to the home of their aunt, where both young ladies had boarded when they had attended Gallia Academy.

◆   ◆   ◆

Several days later, Lizzie was resting on the settee at home when Callie brought her the Thursday *Tribune*. Ordinarily, Lizzie would not take time to read the paper during the daytime, but, with her lame leg, she had to rest often. As she scanned the section for Clay Township's news, she found an account of her accident that surprised her. "Goodness! I had better write to Berte before someone clips this and mails it to him," she muttered to herself. She had already mentioned getting kicked by the horse in her last note, but she had downplayed the incident so Berte wouldn't worry. Now she wrote:

November 30, 1893

My Dear Husband:-

I see by the Tribune where I am confined to my bed and will be for several weeks on account of the horse running away. I haven't been in bed only at night since you went away. My left leg is hurt pretty bad, but now I can go on crutches and hope soon to be able to run as fast as I ever did. It may be longer healing than I expect, but I hope not. The bone is not broken but, I guess, fractured. It was a very narrow risk and frightened me so that I had one of those old nervous chills, but now I am so I can eat three times a day and can help with some of the work. Don't worry about me now for if I get worse, I will let you know. I thought if I had to be crippled until Christmas I would have you come home, but now you had better stay.

Lots of love,

Affectionately, your wife Lizzie

11

Depression

The accident had badly frightened Lizzie. Once the shock had worn off, and things seemed back to normal, Lizzie really thought she was quite lucky to have just hurt her leg. Then she treated it as a temporary inconvenience. The crutches were a bother, but she was certain it would only be a few weeks until she was back on her feet and feeling as good as new.

However, her limb didn't recover as expected. The wound developed an infection, and the pain bothered her more and more. The longer the recovery took, the lonelier Lizzie became. Normally stoic about her aches and pains, now, without Berte to lean on, she felt lost, frightened, and worried. She could put on a brave face in front of her family and guests, but her letters grew increasingly morose.

Ten days after the accident, Lizzie wrote:

December 3, 1893

My Dear Husband:-

It is snowing now after raining all day and all last night. It makes it awful lonely for me when these bad days come, especially when I can't go out of the house at all. My leg is healing some but it is still very painful. I can only walk on my crutches.

I felt like today I would be tempted to write for you to come home, but it would only be an expense, and you couldn't do any good as far as healing my leg. But it would be so much comfort to have you here to wait on me.

I didn't intend to tell you that I was hurt so bad, but when I saw in the Tribune where I was so bad, I thought I had done wrong in not telling you all. I couldn't help but thank my Heavenly Father that He spared us from death, which looked for a while like we would surely meet. I thought of what you had said—that if we never meet again here on Earth, we would meet in Heaven where there would be no more parting. I don't think you need to advise me again about the horses. I don't think I will ever be induced to get in behind any horse but one half dead!

The Lord surely must have some work for me to do to have saved me when death was so near. It would have been all right if He had called me to go, but I would like to stay to be with you and Clair, but then the Lord knows best.

I get so lonely on Sundays here alone. My mind is hardly off you one minute during the twenty-four hours. The other night I dreamt of you being here and we had gone to bed. If you had been here, it couldn't have been more real. I can now almost feel the touch of your lips on my face as you kiss me. When I awoke, Clair had his arms around my neck. But oh! How lonely I felt to find that I had only been dreaming.

I have been knitting some for Christmas presents. I will not attempt to give many, for money is too scarce to make many. I wish I had enough money to send you some to buy a new suit of clothes which I expect you need badly now. I wouldn't want you to buy cheap quality clothes because I think that is an expensive thing to do.

Since my leg has been hurt, I am about in the notion of breaking up housekeeping and going home to stay until I get ready to go to you. But the children there are so noisy, I don't believe I could stand to be there now. I am as nervous as can be anyway. Lida and Sallie were here the other night and stayed overnight. They had a big time. I do think they are as good-for-nothing girls as I ever saw. About all either care for are boys and dresses, and they can grunt worse than I can. I think if I had to be with them very long I would go crazy. I must close.

Why don't you write oftener? I get so lonely when I don't hear from you often.

Lots of Love, Aff. your wife,

Lizzie

A few days later, Lizzie recounted her miseries to herself. Christmas was coming. There was no money to be generous with presents. Clair was still soiling his clothes. Callie was no help whatsoever, and her leg hurt badly. Besides, now her arms pained her from using the crutches. One evening, tired and discouraged, Lizzie tried to cheer herself by using her gold-trimmed pink pitcher and the matching washbasin, usually reserved for company, for cleaning up. Usually, she found a bit of joy just using her pretty set. Not tonight. It failed to brighten her dark mood. Thoughtfully, she splashed her face and washed her hands before finding her pen and paper. She missed Berte so. If only he could come home.

December 8, 1893

My Dear Husband:-

I don't know what makes me feel the way I do tonight, but I feel like you are coming home. I wish it could be, but then you would miss so much of your school, and it would cost so much to come home and back. If I don't get decidedly better in a week, I don't believe I can stand it to have you stay away longer.

There isn't any danger now, but if blood poisoning set in, I couldn't live but a short time. If the Lord should call me, it would be all right although I would like to live to see Clair grown up and you succeeding with your work. While I am in this mood, I will tell you other things. I want you to go on in your work for Christ. Don't give that up now, no matter what might happen. Let Jim and Mary have Clair, and I want you to keep him in clothing. I have written out my will, and you will find it in the upper dresser drawer in a black box.

I am not frightened at the outlook, but I would die so much better satisfied if you were here with me. Of course, no such a thing might take place, and the worst is surely over, but I felt I ought to tell you these things tonight in case I don't have another opportunity.

Neither your mother nor father has been down to see me since I got hurt. I guess they think I wasn't hurt much. I thought at first that it wouldn't amount to much, but from what the doctor said today, it will be some time before it will heal up. Don't worry about it, for if I get much worse, I will telegraph you, and you can borrow some money to come home. Oh, how I wish I could see you tonight and hear you pray just once again.

Mrs. Morris had a little girl baby over there. It came last night.

Ma took Clair up home and kept him today. She gave me some money to have someone care for him another day. He is right good and so careful about not hurting my leg. When he accidentally hurts me, he will come and put his little arms around my neck telling me he feels sorry for me. I am tired and as I didn't sleep much last night, I guess I'll go to bed.

Good night, and may the Lord bless you.

Lizzie

Saturday morning: I feel better today as I slept for the first night since I got hurt. I have just dressed my leg. It looks better this morning. I am so in hopes that the worst is over for I don't want you to have to leave your school until you feel you have gone long enough. Well, the boat is landing. Callie thinks it is you on it. I only wish it were true.

Three days later, Lizzie wrote again. She wanted to be more cheerful, but that was hard to do when she was tired and hurt so badly:

December 11, 1893

My Dear Husband:-

I received two letters and a card from you tonight—how much good it does me to hear from you. I had the doctor examine my leg. He thinks now it will get along all right but will take some time for it to heal. He has been here four times to see me. I sent for him twice. It is not my knee that has been hurting me so, but right on the bone about half way from my knee to my ankle. There is a place cut to the bone about as long as my finger and as wide as two fingers. There is where it gives me the most trouble. I guess the Lord sent it on me as a punishment for not going to you when you wanted me to come so bad.

I couldn't sleep any until the doctor gave me morphine. I tried not to take any last night and slept pretty well until about three o'clock. Then I had to get up and dress my leg. Now don't worry about it, for I will get well some time, and I hope this will make a better woman out of me.

I had a real nice Thanksgiving but stayed here all day long. I was thankful because the Lord saw fit to spare my life a little longer. If only He will spare me to see you once more, I will never—no never—allow you to leave me again.

I asked Ma today if I should ask you to come home. She said that I shouldn't because there is nothing you can do to help my leg heal, and it would just cost so much more money."

Clair said just now to tell Papa to come home and see him and to write him a letter. I tell you he is just a case. He is just wild over Mrs. Morris's baby. He said he was going to tell you to buy him a little baby. He was ready to give his cloak and cap up to the baby. They brought it over for me to see it today. It weighed nine pounds and is so fat. It makes me want one of our own now. I expect I will be tempted strong when I once more get to see you.

Good night, and may the Lord bless you and give you a wonderful success.

Your aff wife, Lizzie

12

Reaffirmation

"Poor Berte." Lizzie was speaking as she poured tea for Rose. "I'm afraid I really frightened him when I wrote that letter when I was so blue. I even told him what to do with Clair when I die. I don't know why I did that except I really do want to see him."

Rose raised an eyebrow. "You wrote that to Berte? Good heavens. He must have been absolutely wild with worry. I know I don't always have the best to say about my brother-in-law, Lizzie, but I do know he loves you dearly. What did he say in his letter?"

"Well, that's when he wrote that he was coming home unless I telegraphed him to stay. He was worried about me, bless his heart. He really wanted to come home to me, and, goodness knows, I wanted him to. There was a lot of confusion about our letters. Evidently, some of them got delayed. I got one that was dated before the one I had already received the week before. By the time I sent my telegram, he had written others. It has been so hard. I still don't know what he will do. Please don't tell Ma and Pa that he's thinking of coming home—or anyone else, for that matter. People have been so hateful about Berte's not sticking to a job. It just makes me feel terrible. I love him, Rose. I really do," her voice caught a little. Quickly, Lizzie swallowed and continued in a stronger voice, "Someday people are going to be able to communicate more easily. They'll have to! Won't those new telephone things be something? It surely would have been grand to have one while we're trying to straighten things out between here and Colorado. I suppose those telephones will be even more expensive than telegrams so they probably will never do us any good.

"Here, let me read you some from his last letters. You'll see just how much my Berte loves me. He writes:

I received your letter today saying not to come. I had made up my mind to come Monday. I haven't much time to wait for a reply because my half fare runs out soon. I suppose it was your letter in which you were so blue that made me feel as though I wasn't doing my duty by you, and that made me terribly homesick...I would have never thought about pulling up and going home if you hadn't been hurt.

"But then, he goes back and forth about what he can do to earn money if he stays, or what he can do to earn money if he comes home. I am really confused, and I think my poor boy is, too. But, oh Rose, he does love me. He does. In one of his letters, he was having a lot of trouble with inkblots. He never was too handy with an ink pen. Anyway, he called all the splotches 'kisses.' Wasn't that sweet? I want to see him so badly." A quick stamp of her foot emphasized Lizzie's feelings. She winced from the stab of pain it caused to her injured leg.

"Oh, Lizzie, of course, you do," Rose comforted her by moving close and touching Lizzie's arm tenderly. "You two just shouldn't have to be separated like you are. Now you must get your leg well so you can join Berte in the spring. You know that then it will be me who is missing you though!" Rose reminded her sister. "You're right. Someday communications will be easier. It surely would be grand if we could just pick up one of those telephones. Telegrams are really too costly. I understand why you can't just send one off every day to get things cleared up. That would cost you a fortune."

"Rose, thank you for coming to call. I need to confide in someone, and Ma and Pa just don't understand how I feel. The rest of the family can be so mean about Berte. Here, let me read you what he said about his calling. Then, you'll understand Berte better, too. But promise me, you'll never let Berte know I shared his letter with you." Lizzie sorted through the little box and pulled out another letter and read aloud from the middle:

> *When your father offered you that farm, I went to work with a cheerful heart. Then when I stood there looking out on the site to build on, my conscience condemned me. I felt that I had done a great wrong in allowing that to tempt me from doing what the Lord had called me to do. I was ashamed of myself because I rebelled so against the Lord for so long. I shrank from my responsibility to preach and tried to persuade myself that I was not called to go preach. Other people couldn't believe that I was called to preach. I believe you felt that way yourself. I'm not sure but what you still feel that way. With all those doubting me, I kind of half believed that I must be mistaken about it myself. This confusion—or rebellion—has almost ruined my health, my mind, body, and every thing else. How useful I might be now had I but surrendered myself to God in the beginning.*

"See, Rose, he had to follow the Lord. That day, a dove appeared to him, sent by the Holy Spirit. And now the Lord has called him to the West. No one else seems to understand."

Rose sat silent for a while. Then she spoke softly, "Yes, Lizzie. I see how much this means to Berte—and to you. I just hope things work out the way you hope. In a cheerful tone Rose continued, "May I have another half cup of tea before I leave? The meringue on your lemon pie is so light and fluffy. Mine always weeps. I guess that's why I'm destined to be an old maid. Lizzie, you're lucky to have someone to write you such letters."

After Rose left, Lizzie pondered why Rose had been so reserved in her response, even changing the subject so soon. But she soon forgot her sister's words as she re-read Berte's words about Christmas:

> *I wish I had enough money to make you a nice present, but I haven't. I will try to make up for it by being good and loving you harder. I may make you a present of myself at Christmas. Would you be satisfied with that present? All I can give you just now is my love.*

I found a new pair of mittens last week. I tried to find the owner all week but couldn't. Then, I was tempted to send them to you, but I decided that if you knew they were "found", you would not wear them. How could I feel good over making a gift that never cost me anything and belonged once to some one else? So, I put them on a stand in the schoolhouse for someone else to find.

Lizzie smothered a laugh. Someone else's gloves indeed! She certainly would have been upset had he sent those to her. But, she did understand. She wanted desperately to send something special to Berte. No gloves or anything else had been found here, or perhaps she would have been tempted to do the same. No matter. Surely they would soon be together. But Berte must not come home now. It was such an expense. She hoped he got her telegram telling him to stay. Well, maybe that wasn't really what she hoped, but she knew in her heart that he should stay and finish his studies.

13

Acceptance

Berte's letters to Lizzie in December reflected his confusion in not knowing what to do. He wrote that he should be home with her yet her letters told him to stay. The mails were slow; telegrams were expensive. Lizzie certainly wanted her husband home, especially for Christmas, but both her mother and her doctor confirmed what she really knew: Berte should stay in Colorado. There was no need for him to return except for their love. Lizzie's leg was healing. It would only take time. One evening, Lizzie stood at the back door gazing at the fading sun. It painted a swath of pink across the aquamarine sky. As she watched, high, wispy, long-fingered pink clouds turned to lavender while the salmon clouds closer to the horizon changed to gold and then to a burnished, glowing bronze silhouetting the hill above the pasture. Lizzie absorbed the peace and beauty of the moment. Serenity washed over her. She went inside to write one of her longest letters to Colorado. It displayed an acceptance and calm that earlier notes lacked:

December 19, 1893

My dear Husband:-

I don't know whether to write you or not. I don't know what to think. In one letter I got last night you said that you would come home unless I telegraphed you to stay. I got one tonight saying you would wait until you heard from me. That letter was dated before the one I got yesterday. I telegraphed you last night to stay for I am getting better (if it is slowly) and as

63

soon as I get well, I am coming to you. You can do as you please, and I would be so happy to see you now, but I think it would be better for you to stay there now. I will promise you faithfully, I will come as soon as my leg gets well.

I want to go west and spend one year anyway. Then I could tell whether I would like it there all the time or not. I do not want to stay in Ohio next year at all. I won't say I will not stay here, but I feel that way sometimes. I think the best plan will be for you to stay there and go to school until conference. Then, if possible, get into the conference there or in Nebraska. Unless you stay this time in the west, I am afraid I will never cross the boundary lines of Ohio.

I feel so sorry for you that you are so homesick, for I have been there myself. When you wrote me last fall that you had refused work, I thought then, my own dear boy, that I couldn't nor wouldn't stand it, yet by the help of my Heavenly Father I did. Now I am glad you went to school first. So, now I think it best you give up coming home, and I will soon be with you again. Then if we are ever so foolish to separate this way again, I hope I may be called to the better world first.

The doctor was here tonight. When I told him why you were coming home, he said it wasn't necessary at all for I am getting along now as well as can be expected. How I would love to see you and have a good talk, but the Lord surely knew best or he never would have allowed this separation for so long. When I got your letter you were coming, I thought I couldn't telegraph you to stay, but then I thought that it was best for your good and the promotion of your work so I acted accordingly and telegraphed you to stay.

Please pray for me that I may be more patient and more faithful.

I must close now and go to bed or no one will get up in the morning. They always wait for me to call them. Wishing you a Merry Christmas.

I remain your affectionate wife, Lizzie

As Christmas approached, Lizzie decided the best way to get over her disappointment that Berte would not be with her was to try to make others happy. Then, she hoped she could forget her lonely life. A cedar tree from the pasture was brought in to decorate. Lizzie popped corn and made balls for the tree. Clair danced as his mother added them to their tree. She found pretty objects around the house to add to it and strung berries into ropes to add to the decorations. By spending only 55 cents of her hard earned pennies to fix up the tree, she was sat-isfied she could make Christmas special for those around her.

Taking an old overcoat of Berte's, Lizzie added cotton batting around the collar and cuff. Then she enlisted Ernie, one of the neigh-bors, to act as Santa Claus. Clair would receive a 2 1/2 cent dog as his main present. Of course, he would also find an orange in his stocking. She would not add a lump of coal although she knew her teasing Berte always did. Her Christmas activities brightened Lizzie's days, and she reveled in watching Clair's joy.

Her gift to Berte was free. She cut a piece of one of Clair's curls and mailed it in an envelope to Colorado. Lizzie had wanted to go to town and have Clair's picture made for Christmas, but her getting hurt had made that impossible, even if she had had the extra cash. Little Clair was growing up. She reported that he told her twenty times a day how much he loved her—especially when she was ready to scold him for something. He loved Mrs. Morris's baby and called it his little sister. Lizzie teased, "I guess we'll have to buy him one for he loves a baby so."

On Christmas Eve, Lizzie drew the old quilt around her and wrote to her husband so far away. She sat at her desk in front of the fireplace with a cup of hot tea steaming beside her.

My dear Husband:-

While I am all alone I will write some to you. Bessie took Clair up home this morning, and I have been alone most of the day. It is a perfectly lovely day. The sun is shining so bright and warm, it makes one think it is spring instead of Christmas time.

I haven't been out yesterday or today any. I don't feel very well. It is noth-ing but what every woman is troubled with. I will soon feel better. I don't know whether it has made my leg hurt more or whether I walked too much yesterday, but my leg hurt last night and today. I don't intend to get dis-couraged again about it. I intend to get well now as fast as ever I can so I can go to you.

I am going to try to get all my work done up the first of next month so then when I get well, I can go right to packing when you say come.

Mrs. Morris's little girl is the sweetest little thing. I guess she intends for me to name it. I wanted to call it Mira, but they didn't like it so I told her the other day to call it Grace. Now I like the name of Alma, so I guess I will go over and tell her that. If they don't like it, I will let you name it. I will name our little girl Mira (if we get one.)

Wishing you a Merry Christmas and a Happy New Year,

Your loving and aff. wife,

Lizzie

14

Christmas

Knocks on the door wakened Lizzie. She pulled on her warm wrapper, shoved her feet into the felt slippers and sleepily opened the front door. Two smiling children from a nearby home stood in the frosty air. It wasn't even daylight yet!

"Morning, Mrs. Ingels. Merry Christmas!" the older girl exclaimed. Then she and her younger brother stood waiting patiently and politely but obviously expecting a Christmas treat.

"My lands of Goshen, children," Lizzie replied. It's way too early to find out if Santa Claus has been here yet. You scoot on home now and give me a few more hours to see if he has left you any treats here." She smiled as she closed the heavy door. Glancing at the wall clock, Lizzie was amazed to discover it was only 4:30 in the morning. "Those little ones are certainly mighty anxious for Christmas," she chuckled as she climbed back under the warm quilts for another hour of napping before it was time to start the Christmas activities.

Lizzie was up and dressed early and had already mixed up a batch of her butterscotch cookies when Clair tottered out of the bedroom. She lifted the sleepy child, gave him a hug, then shifted him to her left hip while she dexterously placed the pan of cookies in the oven, which she had already fired up. There would be just enough time to change Clair and get him dressed before the children's Christmas cookies were ready to come out.

Clair could barely stand still while his mother dressed him. "Did Santa Claus come, Mama? Did he? Did he?" he questioned as his little feet danced in impatience.

"Not yet, my dear. We have to be patient a little while longer. He has many visits to make today, you know. Let's go get your oats and milk. Then, we'll wait for him," Lizzie answered, leading the little boy towards his high chair at the table. Christmas was exciting no matter how old you were, Lizzie thought. If only Berte could be with them, it wouldn't matter how slim Christmas would be this year. But, as far as it was within her power, Lizzie had determined to make this a happy day for her family and friends.

Clair alternately played on the floor with his rag doll and scrambled to the window peering out for a glimpse of Santa. While he was momentarily absorbed with the old doll, there was a commotion at the door. "Ho, ho, ho", roared a voice. When Lizzie opened the door, the wide-eyed little boy stared at the stranger with the fuzzy white beard wearing a coat with white furry stuff on the collar and cuffs. From a big burlap bag, which appeared pretty flat and empty, the stranger pulled two packages wrapped in brown paper and string. "Here you are, Son. Here are your presents for this very special day. If you'll look in your stocking up there on the mantel, you'll find something else." Clair didn't appear to notice the wink directed from the stranger to his mother nor the fact that the cottony beard was slipping. Santa was too much of a wonder.

Ripping open the packages, Clair discovered a set of blocks and the little toy dog. He immediately carried them to a corner of the room and began to play. He built a house with the blocks and put the new dog inside. Lizzie had to remind him to look into his stocking. The little boy was amazed that it held an orange, all for him, as well as some warm butterscotch cookies. "Mama," Clair called, "I like Christmas."

"So do I, Son. So do I," Lizzie said softly, wishing Berte could share their son's joy.

Soon, Santa disappeared, but other family members and neighbors arrived for dinner. Lizzie served roast chicken, fat dumplings and creamy mashed potatoes swimming in rich gravy, corn pudding, warm rolls and strawberry preserves topped off with peach pie. Each found oranges and cookies to take home. They gathered around the little cedar Lizzie had decorated admiring the popcorn strings and the berry clusters. The few candles tied strategically on the tree were lit in honor of the day while everyone sang "Joy to the World" and "Silent Night", enjoying the warmth of family, friends, and hearth. Only Lizzie knew silent heartache that day. Her world was not complete.

15

Frustration

January brought both flurries of snow and flurries of letters between Ohio and Colorado. Lizzie, her leg feeling more normal, was anxious to sell excess furniture, finish her sewing, pack, and leave for Colorado, but the letters she was receiving from Berte vacillated daily between his going home or staying on. Their letters continued to pass each other's in the mail resulting in confusion and frustration as they tried to decide what they should do.

January 7, 1894

My Dear Husband:--

While the children are playing with their blocks I will try to write some to you. I don't feel very well tonight. I don't know what is the matter with me here lately; my stomach, I guess, is out of order in some way. My stomach is sore most of the time, and I am so nervous. If I sit and sew or knit for an hour, I get so nervous I can hardly stand to be still another minute.

There is a lady here on a visit to her mother. She is from Kansas and wants me to be ready to go when she goes home. They say she is a real nice lady, and she will go right through Kansas City so I would have company for over half of the way.

I would like to get ready to go with her. I can get all my sewing done now while I can't walk. Then I will want to pack my things when I can walk. I want you to go to school as long as you think it necessary, but I am still so anxious for you to get down to real work—that is, preaching the gospel. I hope to receive the blessing I have been praying for. I want to live for Christ, not for self.

I have been popping corn, and it makes me homesick to see you for I know how you used to like it. The last two letters you have written have made me more homesick than any others since you have been away. I have made up my mind to get ready to go when my leg gets well and would so much rather you would have work, that is, if you are through with your school. If not, why, of course, I will have to do the best I can.

I do not want you to dress me like a queen, nor do I ask you to provide for an extra grand living. Of course, I like to have things nice but as I know well, we can't live like some of our friends. Yet I would like to have a comfortable living.

I gave Pa the money to pay the taxes. It was $2.53. The ticket agent says the fare from Gallipolis to Denver is $31.10, and there won't be any reduction on price until summer.

Your aff. wife, Lizzie

Two days later, all thoughts of moving were driven from Lizzie's mind. The sound of Clair's screams caused her to turn from the fire she was tending. Clair was running towards the house, his long finger curls flying behind him. His two-year-old steps were tiny, but he pounded towards the safety he sought. When he reached the door where his mother had just emerged, he found solace in the folds of her long skirt. Sobs racked the little body and tears splashed on the front of his white dress and dampened his mother's skirt. Gathered into his mother's arms, the sobs subsided somewhat, and Clair wiped both eyes across his sleeves. He paid no attention to the running nose, but his mother took care of that with the ever-ready handkerchief.

"Clair, dear heart. What has happened? What's the matter?" A cursory examination revealed a cut on Clair's head that was bleeding though not profusely.

Clair reached towards his leg and cried again. "That big old dog bit me. Bad dog. Bad, bad dog," Clair sputtered indignantly. In response to his mother's questions, the story unfolded through diminishing sobs. Clair had been over to Mrs. Morris's to see the new baby and was on his way home when he passed the Murphy's dog at the store. He had kicked at the dog to get him to move off the porch, and the hound bit him on the leg and knocked him against the door, which had caused the laceration on his head.

Lizzie, although an animal lover, at that moment was more concerned for her son's safety than she was in a lecture on cruelty to animals. With an extra squeeze, she nuzzled her son and gently pinched his plump cheeks. In a few moments, Clair rewarded her with a tentative smile.

When Clair was calmed, Lizzie asked Mr. Morris to drive them to the doctor's. She was afraid the poison from the dog bite would make Clair sick. The doctor provided ointment for the wound and soothed her worries. Only after they were home again and Clair was sound asleep for a nap, did Lizzie realize she had left her crutches in the corner by the fire when she ran outside. She guessed her leg must be better if she had been able to negotiate on her own for that time.

In Berte's letter that night, she told the story, careful not to make it worry Berte as much as it had upset her.

A few days later, having heard unsettling news from Berte, she scolded him.

January 11, 1894

My Dear Husband:--

I didn't think I would write to you tonight-but I feel so worried that I don't know what to do. I feel like I cannot stand this strain much longer. Your letter tonight still worries me. I thought you were still in school where I hoped you would stay until you took a circuit. I don't know what to do now. I thought by the time I would be ready to go to you, you would be ready and willing to take a circuit. But I guess I am doomed to disappointment this year sure.

I want to quit keeping house in two or three weeks, but if you don't take work by that time, I don't know if I will go. Of course, if you think you can do better not to take work than to take it, why I suppose that would be best. I am worried nearly to death. This uncertainty is very trying. I some-times think I cannot live much longer this way.

Callie is so provoking that I feel I cannot put up with her insults much longer. She doesn't want to do anything except the cooking and the rest of the time she wants to sew and do for herself. If I want her to do anything for me, she scolds me.

Clair said just now, "I want Papa to come home and see me tonight." He thought those fur things you sent, the muff and mittens, were so pretty. I have been trying to teach him his prayers, but he says "Now you lay me down to sleep." I told him that Jesus doesn't like bad little boys but wants them to be good so they could come and live with him some day. He looks so earnestly at you when you talk to him that way. I think he will either be a very bad boy or an awful good boy, for he will not be a halfway boy. Oh, how I wish you were with us so you could help to train him to be a good boy. There is no little responsibility in training a child. I have tried so hard, but it is hard when others will tell him to say and do things that are not nice. He never hears anything but what some time he will repeat it. He heard "Gee whiz" one day, and in a few days he was saying it several times. I had to punish him like everything for it, but Callie will keep him saying it. At breakfast this morning he told Maggie not to eat all the cakes up. Last night he took the meat plate and put it on the other side of the table to keep Maggie from taking two pieces of meat.

Clair's face is better now. I keep salve on it so it won't leave a scar. He was very brave when the doctor worked on it, and it doesn't bother him any.

Jersey wouldn't eat her feed this morning but ate it tonight. I thought when she didn't eat this morning that I had had a little more than my share of trouble.

Well, I must close and go to bed. Goodnight and may the Lord bless you.

Aff Your wife, Lizzie

It has turned lots colder here today.

A great many are sick around here with the Grippe.

16

Packing

Continuing to make plans for her move west, Lizzie went shopping for a trunk and items she needed for her trip. When Berte wrote that he was now in Colorado Springs, she took the news philosophically. She answered calmly:

I was very much surprised last night when I got your letter saying you are at Colorado Springs. I didn't think you would go down there but thought you would take work on a circuit, but as you didn't do as I wanted you to, I will try and make the best of it and be as contented as I can try to think it best.

Then she chided him gently that he was as bad as Clair, both doing whatever they wanted, no matter what she thought. All she planned to ship was her sewing machine and Clair's rocking chair, bedclothes, and one carpet.

Berte's next letter showed concern for her health:

I will promise to wait on you. I know it will take a good deal of my time to do housework, but I am so anxious about your health. I think you will be better here. I am afraid Callie doesn't prepare food very well, or it may be the worry that causes your dyspepsia. I think I can doctor you up with our new Hygiene. If you can't live here, we can go back. There are lots of people here who are nervous. This is a beautiful climate. People who have gone back east can never be satisfied after they have been here, they say. May the good Lord help you to get well and help you to come to me.

But a week later, Lizzie was fretting again, afraid that Berte was on his way home before she could get ready for the move. Her boxes were ready, a new dress and two aprons were ready to pack, and just as soon as she finished her sewing, she would be ready to pack. She implored Berte to tell her immediately if he were coming home so that she would be spared the packing.

By January 31, Lizzie had begun packing in earnest. Her letter again demanded her husband's intentions:

...now I want to know at once what you intend to do. Do you want to come home or do you want to stay there? I do not intend to pack another thing until I hear from you, and then I will do what you say, and you must forever hold your peace. One letter I get, you don't want to stay, and I make up my mind to stay. Before I can get anything done, you want me to come right off, and by the time I get some things ready, you say for me to stay here. Now if you want me to stay, I want you to say so and be done with it. I am so worried tonight I don't know what to do. If I had you here, I would box your ears good for being so unsettled.

The letter continued her tirade, born of frustration, and threatened that if she ever did get to Colorado, she intended to stay. If he didn't want to, then he could just get a divorce because she planned to stay at least three years even if she died there.

By February 4, Lizzie was concerned about the state of the roads. Heavy snow followed by rains had mired the roads. Now it would be such a task to move anything. She reported her recent doctor's visit for a check up on her heart. The doctor had told her that her heart was fine, but that the spells she had been having were caused from stomach trouble. Berte had relieved her when he had written about the possibility of a charge in Nebraska. Her hopes were up that soon she would join him in the west. Lizzie continued to report her travel plans,

---

I have made up my mind now to ship the bedding, carpets, and dishes to you as soon as I hear where you are going to stay. About one week after I ship them I will start myself. I would rather not go at one certain time. You may guess the reason why. That will be in a week from next Friday. I don't fear to travel alone now. Guess I won't take the sleeper for it will cost me so much more. Well, I will stop now and get some coal in for the night…

Emotions soared to the heights and then crashed again. Yet Lizzie still hoped. A series of letters reveals her determination to join him and her frustration with the delays.

February 18, 1894

My Dear Husband:--

I am happy this morning because I got a letter from you last night saying you were better and the prospect for you getting a place was better. The past week has been a very trying one to me. I felt like I was forsaken by God and humanity.

When I received your telegram telling me you were coming home, I was almost crazy. I felt like if you did come home I never would go out of the house again nor would I ever speak to anyone. You must not think I don't love you nor want to see you, for I do. That is the reason I hate to hear folks talk about you, and you know they would if you came home.

Now please take either place the Elder may see fit to place you and that right at once so I can leave here. I have always wanted to go west and will never be satisfied until I do. I have nearly everything packed and so many things sold that it will be better for you to stay there now and let me come. I will not stay here. I can stand a great deal, but patience ceases to be a virtue sometimes.

When I got your telegram that you were coming, I couldn't say anything to anybody. I just got ready and went to town that night. I stayed from Tuesday evening until Friday afternoon and looked for you every time the Columbus train came in. Now please write me as soon as you get this about where I am to stay. If you love me at all, please do make up your mind to stick to one thing and let me go to you. I am worn out now

*answering people, 'I don't know when I am going.' Please lighten my bur-
den. I am so worried that I am almost down sick this morning.*

Aff Your wife Lizzie

February 19, 1894

My Dear Husband:--

*I received your card today asking me for more money. Now I have sent you
$40 since you left Denver and have done without things that I need to do
so. I haven't any money now to send you at all. If you need money, you
must go to work and earn some.*

*I will not send you any to come home on for it will do no good for I do not
intend to stay here, and I want you to quit worrying me so about your coming home. I have done nearly everything to help you to go and see the
world and have a good time. Now it is my time. I have never been outside
Gallia County since we were married.*

*Last spring I wove carpets and tried to save enough to go to the World's
Fair and was disappointed in that. And then I thought, of course, I would
go west last fall and was disappointed in that. And now I had thought, of
course, you wouldn't disappoint me this time and would surely stay there
so I could go west. Now, alas, in that I see that I am doomed to be disappointed. I do not think I have been selfish.*

*I will just say now that I am going west this spring and you may do just as
you like. You can come to your father's and stay, and I will make my own
living in some way. I will take Clair with me. I will leave here in two weeks,
and if you want to ever see us again, you will have to stay there and make
a home for us. If you don't, I will take the baby and go where I am not
known and make my own living. I know the Lord will surely provide for us
in some way. I don't think he has forsaken me, too. But as far as earthly
friends are concerned, there are very few. No one does truly love me but
Clair. He seems to feel that I am lonely and forsaken and tries to fill the
gap, but I long for more than he can give.*

*I feel like life is such a burden that I would be willing to go to my grave if it
weren't for Clair. But a motherless boy has such a hard and joyless life that
I feel I can't leave him here all alone. But God will care for him, and I pray*

that he will make him a good boy, and he will grow up a true Christian and go to Heaven when he dies.

I am about sick tonight. Worrying hurts me lots worse than work does, and the past week has been an unusually hard one for me. My leg has been hurting me a great deal for two or three days; I am afraid I will have trouble with it again if I have to be on it as much as I have had to be. Well, I must stop and sew carpet rags so Mrs. Morris can help weave it next week

Your wife Lizzie

February 20, 1894

My Dear Husband:--

Your card received in which you were going to locate at that place. Please accept the offer and stay there. Find a house right away, a small house with not more than two or three rooms. We can do with little room. Please be settled this time so I will know what to do. I expect I was a little hard in my last two letters, but I was almost wild. I will have to rest now pretty soon.

Your aff wife, Lizzie

The packing continued.

17

Settled

Outside the sun shone brightly, and the air was soft with the promise of spring in the Ohio Valley. Lizzie had opened windows to air the house so that it would be fresher for the new tenants. She wore an old but freshly ironed apron over her skirt and shirtwaist and hummed as she swept the floor with her broom.

"Clair," she called. "Please come pick up your blocks and little dog for Mama. They need to go in that box right there for our big trip." Clair skipped over and, one by one, tossed his favorite playthings in the box. His mama's big trunk was standing near the door. It was filled and locked. Only a few pieces of furniture were still in place in the parlor.

"Now, we need to get your face washed and a clean dress on you, Clair. Just as soon as I finish redding up the sitting room, we're going to ride over to your Grandma and Granddad's house for dinner to say "Good-bye" before we leave to see your father at the end of the week."

"Chug, chug. Choo choo," chanted Clair, making the block travel like a train in the air, as he submitted to his mother's ministrations with washcloth and comb. Then, he was off and out the door followed by admonitions not to get dirty again.

As Lizzie was pulling off her apron and glancing in the mirror at her own hair, Clair came running back into the house. "Mama! Mama! Come quick. There's a man outside."

Puzzled, Lizzie made her way towards the door. No one was supposed to pick her up. She had planned to drive herself and Clair up home. The tall man was climbing down from the wagon, his back to her. Her heart jumped as she recognized the broad shoulders. It was her Berte. She ran to him, and he hugged her and swung her off her feet. Then Berte reached down to ruffle his little son's hair. Clair seemed shy. Six months ago, he had been still a baby when his father left. He didn't seem to recognize the man in front of him.

"Oh, Berte, Berte. You're home!" Lizzie cried. She kissed him chastely on the lips when he hugged her tightly to him. Then she led him into the house, their fingers intertwined. Berte stooped to lift Clair and soon had the little boy laughing as he swung him towards the ceiling. Lizzie turned away from them, her eyes veiled in tears. Her hand lightly caressed the trunk standing near the door. Reaching into the still opened box, Lizzie retrieved Clair's toys and set them on the floor. She swallowed hard, blew her nose, wiped the back of her hand across her eyes, tucked her handkerchief back in her sleeve, and then joined her husband and son at play.

"Are you hungry?" she asked.

Post Script

When she was clearing her home, my mother handed me an old wooden jelly box filled with fragile, brittle letters. As I carefully sorted through them and read a few, my eyes grew wide. "Mother, these are fantastic. They should be made into a book." Mother grew quiet and said, "No, I don't think so. They are so private."

The letters, carefully saved by my grandmother, chronicle her teen years until after her marriage. They range from family letters from her grandmother, from her friend who had moved to the Dakota Territory, to those between herself and her fiancée, Berte Ingels, as they planned their marriage. And then there is this collection, which tells a complete story. The bulk of this collection, however, was in her handwriting—those letters saved by Berte when he was in Nebraska and Colorado. He, ever the romantic of the two, had saved nearly all of her letters and carefully shepherded them back to Gallia County where Lizzie took possession and stored them with her others. Interestingly, the courtship letters contain plea after plea, from both of them, to destroy the letter after it is read—yet someone kept them.

I knew three of my grandparents. I visited my other grandparents regularly, but Lizzie died when I was four. Berte then lived with us until he died the week I graduated from high school. My only memories of my grandmother revolve around sitting next to her bed coloring and playing with paper dolls. I have vague recollections of trips to the farm before that when Mother drove daily to take care of her ailing mother. And yet, through these letters, I KNOW Lizzie. I see her in my mother. I see her in me. I see her in my daughters. She is us, and we are her. I know the way she thought, the way she felt, and the depth of her devotedness to her husband, her children, and her God. Through her words, our souls have touched. That we share a name makes her story even more real to me. Named for her and married to Ralph Riggs, gives me now her maiden name. Although we have not found a connection between the two families yet, it has given us an incentive for more genealogical work.

Other treasures of my grandmother's written word include a careful collection of botanic samples in a scrapbook made for Gallia Academy classes and a journal Lizzie made which describes the ending of her high school years and two long trips on the Ohio. When I read of her wish to write about HER ancestors after that trip up the Ohio to Matamoras, I felt I had her blessing to write her story for her descendants. Her hand guided my pen. Contrary to my mother's feelings, I think Lizzie saved her letters so that we could know her. Edited excerpts from Lizzie's journal are included in Appendix A that follows. They reveal the day-to-day living in those times, from high school life to work on the farm to social visits to life on the river-boats.

◆   ◆   ◆

After his return to Ohio, Berton ran a little store, was a postmaster, and did marginal farming. He never became an ordained minister although he did have a lay preacher's license. He carried his faith with him like a mantle until his death. His last word as he died was, "Hallelujah!" Berte's letters, carefully saved by Lizzie, record their courtship and engagement. Although they lived probably less than 15 miles from each other at the time, the mail was the means of communication. These early letters show Berte's romanticism. Appendix B contains his letters.

Lizzie finally did make trips to Colorado. Letters from her to Berte, back in Ohio, appear a few years later when she evidently visited family in the West. Brother Truman Riggs in 1898 and sister Laura Frances joined Everett Clair in 1902. Mary Mildred joined the family in 1904. No Mira, Grace, or Alma appeared. In 1927, Lizzie made another trip west to take her daughter Frances for treatment for tuberculosis. It was unsuccessful. Frances died in young adulthood. She left behind a two-year-old son. Earlier, Clair had also died, tragically young, and never knew his unborn daughter. The deaths devastated the close-knit family.

Celicia Elizabeth Riggs married Berton H. Ingels in 1889 when she was 25 years old. She died in 1942 at the age of 78 after a series of strokes. Berton lived to be 90 and died in 1955, still straight and tall. They are buried together at Mound Hill Cemetery in Gallipolis overlooking the river they had lived on all their married life.

◆   ◆   ◆

The letters that appear in this book remain true to Lizzie and Berte's words. Spelling and punctuation and minor points of grammar were changed when necessary for clarity. Some letters are combined or have left out details that are confusing, redundant, or unrelated to their story, but the words that appear in italics were basically their own. Some names other than family members have been altered. The narration, which includes descriptions of Lizzie's thoughts and feelings is the work of my imagination, but it was based on my mother, Mildred's, stories about Lizzie and my mother's own personality, which must have mirrored her mother, Lizzie's. Both fiercely independent, they militantly believed in a strong family life. Both worked diligently for their church; both valued family heirlooms. Neither could dream of a life without her husband.

In today's world, when marriages evaporate at the slightest provocation, Lizzie and Berte's story reveals the strengths needed to forge a lasting union. Their faith in God and their love and acceptance for each other, despite trials of separation and financial worries, bonded them for over fifty years. It is a lesson for us all.

Appendix A

Excerpts from The Journal of Lizzie Riggs, 1895

W hen the New Year rolled around in 1885, Lizzie Riggs began a journal of her eventful year. The entries from January through June chronicle her life as a senior at the Gallia Academy in Gallipolis, Ohio. Lizzie lived with her family on a farm seven miles down the Ohio River from Gallipolis. To complete her education, it was necessary for her to take room and board in town. Nearly every weekend she was able to go home to her family. Every Monday morning, often delayed by weather, she made her way, usually by boat, back to her school life.

The entries reflect the social and educational customs of the times. Visits were commonplace and unannounced. Sometimes there were 10 or more extra folks at the dinner or tea table. Gentlemen came to call; ladies called on one another; whole families with oodles of babies came to stay. There were hotels, but who had money to spare when friends and family were available?

Lizzie suffered greatly from headaches. They are mentioned over and over again in her diary. She had her long hair cut very short because the doctor hoped that the headaches might be relieved. They were probably migraine or allergy-related.

Marnie was Lizzie's best friend. Her brothers Ed(d), Jim, and Ernie are often mentioned as well as her married sister Jessie who lived within a long walking distance of Lizzie's town home. Rose was an older sister who lived at home with her parents. The frequent mention of going to get Virgil does not refer to a brother or cousin but rather, evidently, a shared copy of their Latin textbook.

Students today will be amazed to read about the essay that Lizzie presented as part of her high school graduation requirements. It seems to have been the equivalent of a master's thesis, at least as far as preparation time for it. Appendix C contains one of Lizzie's essays. Rehearsals for graduation and the pomp and circumstance of the weeklong ceremonies point out the importance of an education in those days.

Lizzie followed the custom of the day in journal writing, using initials to refer to companions. Sometimes it is difficult to determine the person she is discussing. The lack of punctuation in her original writing coupled with a lack of capitalization made it difficult to determine where one thought ended and another began. She was writing for herself and used a type of shorthand. I have made whatever corrections were necessary, for easier reading; however, the words you read are really Lizzie's. When some words were indecipherable, a blank appears. Let Lizzie tell you her story.

◆   ◆   ◆

The Academy 1895

Jan. 1 After a night of restlessness, arose early to prepare for company. I was looking for Henry, Nettie, and Ida for dinner. They never came so went over to Will Graham's for dinner. Had a real nice time. Mr. and Mrs. C...Marnie, Jim, and I were all that were there. I came home early, worked on my dress, popped corn for supper and went over to Marnie's to get the copy of Virgil. I went to bed late.

Jan. 5 Got up early to come up on boat, but Mamma said I would have to stay at home for I was not well enough to come by land and the river was so full of ice the boat did not come up. Saw the *Telegraph* coming. I went down and got on her. I felt miserable on such a boat with school clothes on. I had my hair all cut off. I have a terrible headache. Had a letter from Will L.

Jan. 6 Went to school. Every one came to see my hair. I went to church. They had a splendid meeting.

Mon 19 The boat never came along until late so never got up here until after 1 o'clock. The water was up in the lane so they had to bring us over in skiff. Uncle Will came up on the *Telegraph* this morning. H came up as we were just finishing breakfast. I went to church this evening, but I had such a cold did not enjoy the meeting much. I came home early and never went to school on Monday.

Thu Jan 22 Went to school. Herbert Ingles stayed all night here last night. I had to get breakfast this morning. I wrote to Edd and finished my essay. Marnie and I did not retire until late.

Fri Jan 23 After a night of wakefulness from coughing, I got up late. I went to school and stayed until after Virgil. Then I went to church but did not stay but one hour. They had a good meeting. I went to school this afternoon. Didn't get to go home today for the river is full of ice. I feel very bad and am very sore from coughing so much.

Sat Jan 24 Never got up until after seven o'clock. Went downtown, scrubbed the kitchen, ate our dinner, and then dressed to go over to Mr. Gilman's. When we saw that Jim had come up horseback for us, we got already to go home and went down to the lower end of town. Then Marnie decided we hadn't better go. So we started to go to George's by going the lower road. We wandered over the hills for about two hours and were not any nearer than when we left town. We then came back to our room, took a fresh start, and got there before supper. I fell down twice and once going out. We were very muddy when got there. Jessie and Baby were both real sick. Never retired until late.

Mon Jan 26 Went to school. Berte came in this A.M. Jim did not come. Worked on Mamma's hood. George was in. Jessie and Baby are better.

Wed Jan 28 Went to school. Mamma and Papa came up this evening and brought us something to eat. They are going out to Jessie's. M and P went sleigh-riding with Henry G. Was only out half hour. Went over to Jessie H.'s to get Virgil. Wrote to Ernie.

Fri Jan 30 Felt bad all day. Colored some ribbon for Mamma's hood and tie for Marnie. Went over to M. to get Virgil. Helped Mrs. Crooks take the baby home this morning.

Tues Feb 3 Came up on the *B. T. Enos*. Felt very lonely. Anna B. was on her. Never got up here until eleven. Went in past Anna . She would not speak; it made me feel so bad. Couldn't hardly keep from crying all afternoon. I heard that she had heard that I had been talking about her which is a big lie for I have not. I think the person that told her such has little to do. I spoke to her this evening coming home from school and told her that I hadn't said what she had heard. I would find out who the tattler was if it wouldn't cause a fuss in our class. Went to see Dr. about my head. He asked me all kinds of questions. Had three letters today. Jessie H came over to get Virgil. My head hurts considerable. Have not heard from Jessie G.

Fri Feb 6 Went to school. Mama and Bessie came up to go out to see Jessie. Went home on boat. Manta got off the boat with us. The river was nearly full of ice. Ada came over and stayed all night with me. Sue went to the Burg to church.

Mon Feb 9 Came up on the boat. Jack took me to the river. It was raining very hard. I almost got lost in the mud when we went down the hill. Got a letter from Will. He was angry because I did not put any beginning in the letter I wrote to him. It made me angry for a while. Then I became very cross for the remainder of the day.

Thur Feb 12 Went to school. Never came home for dinner. When we came home in the afternoon, found Rose and Mary here. They wanted to go home and had sent Jim to hunt a way to go down. They came in on the train last night and stayed all night with Jessie. M. and I went down home with them in a skiff. There was so much ice in the river we were afraid we wouldn't get home again. When we got down to the mouth of the creek, us girls got out to walk the rest of the way home. We were so cold. They were greatly surprised to see us. Mr. C. and Mr. T. stayed all night here.

Fri Feb 13 Never got up until late. Mr. T asked me for my address so he could send me some flowers for my Herbarium. Thanked him for his kindness and gave him my address. Marnie, Jim, Rose and I walked up to Aunt C. for dinner. Had splendid time. Stopped to see Aunt M as we were coming home. Stopped a while at M. Ate apples, potatoes, and popcorn. Went to bed early.

Sat Feb 14 Helped with the work. Baked a cake. Fixed my dress.

Mon Feb 16 Jim brought us up in the sleigh. It was rough in some places. It was very cold coming up. I feel terrible bad about something. Don't know what is getting the matter with me of late.

Thu Feb 19 Went to school. Came home at noon. Dick B. came up after the folks. M and I walked up to the train. No one came. Stopped at Mrs. Ecker's. Went down street. Went up to the train at 9 o'clock. No one came. Don't see why they don't come. Jim and Dick went home.

Fri Feb 20 Went to school. Jim came up after the folks. M, J and I went to train this PM. No one came. Marnie, Jim, Jessie H, and I went out to Jessie G's. Stayed until almost eight o'clock. Came in town. Went to the train. All but Aunt Sallie came. The first person I saw that I knew was Will L.. 9 in all went down in the sleigh. Got very cold before got home. It was 11:30 o'clock when we got home. W. didn't like my hair cut.

Sun Feb 22 One year ago today since we laid Sister Laura in the silent grave. O! What one year of grief and temptation. I long to be with her in her happiness. Sick all day. Felt terrible bad. Was only out of the house once all day. Reube and Marnie came in for a while this evening. All went to church excepting Edd M, Edd B, Bessie, and I. Edd B went to bed early. W. came home from church early. I told him that we had better quit our nonsense. He felt very bad when I told him about my health. It made me feel very bad. I think he cares more for me than I thought. I wish our lives were different. He told me of his intentions of going either to Col. or Cal. He has told Rose about our affair. Heard someone coming. Went to bed.

Feb 23 Will looks very bad this morning. Uncle A brought us up in sleigh. It was real cold.

Feb 24 Went to school. Feel badly. Took examination in Virgil.

Feb 26 Went to school. Worked from 8:50 AM until 2 PM on my paper. Went down to the boat to go home. After we had been there a short time, Jim C. came down after us to go home by land. Will Graham came home this P.M. Will L was surprised to see me looking so well. Went to church. A good many here to stay all night. W is very much discouraged with his Christian life. Feel sorry for him.

Mar 1 Went to Sunday S. More there today have ever has been since last summer. A good many here for dinner. Reube here all day. Received note from W. Feel so sorry that I have treated him the way I have. Felt so bad did not go to church. W was converted. He came home so happy. Several here to stay all night.

Mar 6 Went to school. Got excused to go home this morning. Will came in to go home on the boat. He was real distant towards me. Had a severe spell of headache all day. They had Jubilee day at the church. Felt too bad to go. A good many here for dinner. W was kind enough this afternoon. Never went to church this evening. Took care of the babies while the rest went. They closed the meeting tonight. Felt miserable.

M 7 Helped with the work. Read some of my essay. Knit a pair of socks. Am very sick.

M 11 Was real sick in the night. Feel better this morning. Walked out to Jessie's. She is much better than when last saw her. Bessie and Rob S. was down to spend the evening. Didn't enjoy his company much.

M 12 We were only one hour 5 min walking in the morning. Were afraid R.S. would overtake us. Anna came up this evening to get Virgil. Went to bed late.

M 14 Helped some with work. Read on my essay a great part of the day. M and I went down to see Mr. Crooks this evening after our essays. He gave me great encouragement about mine. I feel as though I could write it now without much difficulty. W found me in the parlor playing. I feel sorry for him. He told me of his intentions of leaving on Monday or Wednesday

M 16 Came up on the boat. Am sick, lonely, and every thing else is the matter with me. I am not fit for any thing. Went to school.

M 20 Went to school. Had an exam. It was very hard. I think it wicked to make such a hard examination. Went home of the boat. W met us at the river. Went down to Mr. Crooks. Am sick. Have a fever blister on my lip. W. heard something that made me very mad. Someone has been reading my letters.

Ap 1 This is called All fools day. Last night had the hardest spell of headache that I ever had in my life. Feel terrible mean and bad today. Had examination in Virgil.

Ap2 Went to school. Papa was up. Went to both skating rinks this P.M. Have the headache again this evening. Worked on essay.

Ap 3 Went to school. Went home on boat. Raining very hard. Got wet. Got off boat. Ernie met me at the river with a horse.

Ap 4 Grandma is better. Helped some with the work. Marnie came over and we worked on our essays most all day. Jessie helped M a great deal with hers but pays as little attention to mine as though she didn't care whether it was fit for a dog to listen to. Went to bed with headache.

Ap 5 Grandma is about the same as yesterday. Cousin Mary and babies came down today. Willis was christened today. There were only thirteen babies here for dinner. Mr. Cook and family here again today.

Ap 6 Came up on the boat. Jessie, baby, Cousin Mary, and four babies I took a baby and walked back in the cabin. I felt so cheap. A lady asked me how old my baby was. I felt so mean. I feel so sorry for Cousin to travel with all the babies. She will leave for NY some-time this week. Never got up here until noon. Went to school this P.M.

Ap 9 Went to school. Mr. Gilman sent horse and buggy around for M and I to go out to Jessie's. It was a very cold drive.

Ap 10 Came in town early and went to school. The boat will not go down until 12 o'clock. We were just starting over to Mrs. Eckers when we met Jim R. M and I went home with him in buggy. Grandma a great deal better.

Ap 11 This is Jessie's birthday. Helped with the work. M came over. We worked on our essays. I have mine ready for corrections.

Ap 14 Went to school. Received letters from Denver and Co this morning and one from Anna G this PM. Copied a page of my essay over. Anna S here for supper.

Ap 17 Went to school. Raining very hard. Went down home on the boat. Went down town after some things before going home. Rose and Aunt Sallie came up today to get Marnie and my dresses for commencement. It was raining hard when we started for the boat. Rose and Aunt Sallie will not go home today. Three years ago today Marnie and I were in Ironton.

Ap 18 Helped Mary with chamber work. Grandma is getting better slowly. Fixed my cloths. Marnie was over this P.M. We made us each a bustle for commencement. Rose came home. Brought me the lovliest dresses, one white embroidered suit and the other black silk.

Ap 19 Went to S.S. Had the headache so bad did not stay for church. Wrote a letter to W. Answered one question that was asked four weeks today. Was so nervous couldn't be still this P.M. O: what is the matter with me! Went over to the graveyard. It always makes me feel so bad and lonely. Was talking to Jim about my essay. It made me feel so bad had to be a little baby about it.

Ap 23 George sent me in the buggy now to school. Anna was sick and went home yesterday. Gave Mrs. C my essay to correct. Studied our lessons for Monday.

Ap 25 Did not sleep hardly any all night with my head. Was very sleepy when the bell rang. Worked on my blue silk. Almost finished it. Went down to Mrs. Crooks to the social. Didn't have a very good time. Good many there. Got a letter from Anna S. She is not much better. She does not know when she will come back to school. Never went home from parsonage until 10 o'clock.

Ap 26 Went to S.S. and Church. Wrote to CW after dinner. Wrote the longest letter ever wrote in my life. 16 pages, then all over the corners. M. Hay here this P.M. Went a piece with her.

Ap 27 Came up on the boat. Jim R got here just as were coming up from the boat. M and I went over to the school house. They didn't have any school today. We started home. Found Jim. Went up to see Anna S. Drove down to Bell's after my hat. Went over to hear their pieces at school house. They have not fixed any so nice as this is. Gram's 63 birthday is today which they are celebrating. Jim took M and I to hear the "boy orator". It was not what I expected yet it was real good for a boy of fourteen years.

Ap 28 Went to the P.O. Marnie got letter from Brown. He wishes to be married before September. I hope her father will be prudent enough to not let her. Went to school. Met Anna's sister Bell. She said that A was no better. I am afraid she will never be able to come back to school. I feel so very lonely this P.M. Wish I could get a letter. Went over to the P.O. Got letter from C. It made me feel so bad, had to take a good cry. Jessie H came over. We went down to Mrs. Hardin to call. I felt so bad about that letter. He was out of humor because I had said "no". Answered it this evening.

May 1 Helped with the work. Worked on my silk dress. Finished the skirt. I wish I had never tried to graduate.

May 2 Helped with the work. Rose and I made a dress for Bessie. Finished my silk. Mrs. Thomily died this P.M.

May 3 Feel terrible blue this P.M. Grandma Lattin came on the boat last night. Several here today for dinner. Marnie and Miss Williams here this P.M. Have a terrible headache.

May 4 Came up by land. Went to school. Marnie went home to have her dresses fit. Wrote to Ann S. George came in. I went home with him, practiced my essay, then more callers there.

May 7 Went to school. After school we went over to the P.O. I received a long letter from C. We walked out to Jessie's. When we got there, she had gone down home so we walked back. Found her at Mr. Gilman's. We were very tired. Went to bed. C. wrote such a good letter. Asked forgiveness for writing that last letter.

May 8 When got up this morning was very tired and almost sick over walk. Was most too much for me. Mama came up after us. Miss W went down with Marnie and Jim. We had examinations in Algebra today. I got 100.

May 9 We got up early to get work done before 7 o'clock. Miss W came over to work on my dresses. We got a great deal done to them today. Sewed nearly all day.

May 11 Marnie and I came up with Clara G. in the buggy. I got some things and started home with C before noon. Rose and Miss W had my dresses already to try on. Am very tired. Went to bed early. Miss W went over to Aunt S to stay all night.

May 14 Went to school. Walked out to Jessie's. Rehearsed my essay. Went to bed early

May 15 Jessie brought us in this morning. Went to school house. There wasn't scarcely any one there so they dismissed school early. Went over to Mr. G to see the procession. Henry took us a buggy ride. We went up to the show grounds. Papa came up in the carriage after us.

May 16 Didn't do much of any thing but help paper sitting room. Am very tired and have terrible headache.

May 17 Went to SS and C. Wrote to C. Several here this P.M.

May 20 Got up early. Jessie and George are going down home today. We came in the buggy with J. The horse backed over the ditch with us as we were leaving the gate. I was frightened almost to death.

May 21 Went to school. Marnie and I went down and had our pictures taken. I think they are real good. I went back to school house to practice my essay to Mr. C. Am very tired.

May 24 went to SS and C. A great many there. It is Memorial Day. Henry, Ida, Mr. Gilman came down. Henry brought Marnie and me up and Jim R, Ida, and Nettie. We went to hear Dr. DeAest lecture. It was real good. Wish I could go tomorrow night. Henry had to come home with me, of course.

May 25 I have terrible headache. Went to school. Was sleepy all day. Came home feeling so bad had to lie down. Sent a box of cake to C.

May 26 Went to school. Studied for examination in Astronomy.

May 27 Went to school. Heard that I was first on the program. It made me feel so very bad. Wished they had not put me there. Had a long talk with Mr. Hand about it. He said he wanted me there because my essay was so good.

May 28 Went to school. Took examination in Algebra. It was very hard for me. I stayed until all the rest of the class had gone home. I felt so bad about it because I did not get perfect in it. Studied until late for examination in Astronomy. Got letter from C.L. It was a very short one. It made me out of humor. I think by the next letter I get from him that it will be the last. I don't care much whether I do or not. I told Marnie something. She was very much surprised.

May 31 Feel terrible bad this noon. Did not go out of the house until after dinner. Came up to town, dressed in my black silk and new hat and went to church. The class had to march in. I felt better this evening. Mr. May preached.

Jun 1 Did not have to go to school today so straightened up our things. Edd came up and took dinner with us. Went to the Opera House to practice this P.M. Called on Mr. John Gilman's this evening.

Jun 2 Went to the Opera House early to practice. A dog took after us. It frightened us so we were afraid to go out of the house without some of the boys with us. Took our last and final examination in Virgil. It was very hard. Took supper at Mrs. Ecker's. Had nice time. Called at Mrs. Hill's and Mrs. Hamilton's. Had quite a nice time. Went to bed early.

Jun 3 Went over to the Office to see Mr. Hand. Received our programs this A.M. Went to dinner at Mr. John Gilman's. Had nice time. Rose, Gma R, Ada,and Aunt Sallie came up today. Called on Dr. Payne this P.M. Like him ever so much. The class went as a body. Went to the lecture given by Dr. P for our class. It was splendid. His subject was "Sham." It was very late when we got home. I wore my blue silk.

Jun 4 Was at the Opera House a greater portion of the day fixing up things. Was at Mr. Henry Gilman's for dinner. Rode around in the buggy with Gma. Was very tired but had to dress and go down to Mrs. Hamilton's for supper. Rose, Aunt S, Uncle A, Marnie, and I were there. Dressed and went to the Opera House. The doors were opened when we got there. I felt so nervous about being first but when I had read my essay, I was so very glad that I could have shouted for joy. Received a great many pretty flowers and a handsome album. It was very late when we came home. Received a great many good compliments. I am so glad it is all over. Had letter from C.

Jun 5 Did not get up until late. Did not sleep one bit well. Ate our breakfast, then dressed in our suits and went down to the gallery. They say our pictures are good. Went to Mrs. Hill's for dinner and had nice time. Went to Mrs. Williamson's to our reception. Had tolerably good time. Would rather have stayed at home and gone to bed. It was real late when we came home. Bade farewell to our schoolmates.

Jun 6 Got up late but commenced to tear up our rooms and pack our things. Cleaned all the rooms. Jim came up in the wagon to move the things out. Went over to Jim's to wait until Ed was ready to go home. I went to the festival. Had a real nice time, considering how very tired and sleepy I was. Reube was there.

Jun 7 Went to S.S. Was so warm did not stay for C. Jessie and George were here. Went over to Will's this evening.

Jun 8 Was tired but helped with the work. Helped to wash some.

Jun 9 Got up early. Helped iron until my hands had almost blistered. M. and I called on D…and her cousin. Went down after the mail.

Jun 10 Worked on my dresses. Had company for tea. Had a very pleasant P.M.

Jun 11 Rose went to town. Sewed all day. Am very tired.

Jun 12 Sewed most of the day. Marnie and I went over to Clara's this evening. Uncle Charles and Aunt came down this evening.

Jun 13 Helped with the work. Finished my dress

Jun 14 Today is Children's Day so we did not have any S.S. There were more at the church than there has been for some time. Several here for dinner. Aunt and Uncle went to Swan Creek this P.M. Vaughn Hay here for dinner.

Jun 15 Helped with house work. Am very tired. Mr. Ewing came in the little boat. Marnie was over.

Perhaps it was a graduation present. Perhaps Lizzie was going along to help her grandmother get her Aunt Nancy to come home with them. Whatever the reason, Lizzie accompanied her Grandmother Mary Bare Riggs on a steamer trip up the Ohio, apparently past Marietta and probably on first to Hannibal where some of the Bares lived and then back down to New Matamoras which had been founded in 1799 by Lizzie's Great-great grandfather, James Riggs. No Baresville or Bearsville appears on today's Ohio map. Stops along the way to visit cousins are not named. Uncle Squire might have lived across the river in Raven Rock, West Virginia, or he might have lived closer to Little Hocking, Ohio, where Frank lived at some point. My guesses here are based on genealogical information I have.

Lizzie seems bored with much of the trip and is often homesick and/ or ill with her dreaded headaches. However, she enjoyed the company of her relatives and their friends and was happy when she was calling or being called upon. She was awed at seeing where her ancestors had lived and wished she could write their story. That she wished she could write about her ancestors gave me courage to write hers. It had to have been an adventure to this young lady with such wanderlust. Life back on the farm would look pretty monotonous when she returned home.

◆   ◆   ◆

River Journey

Jun 16 Got up early. Commenced to help iron. Took Grandma and Bessie down to the burg. Got a letter from C. He has his shoulder broken. I feel so sorry for him. Will Le came on the Cin evening boat. He is looking bad. Did not get to talk to him much for our boat came along real early. We got on the boat at 8:30 P.M. Miss

Donavan came on at Thomily's landing. Am very tired. Will retire early.

Jun 17 We were just above Pomeroy when we arose from almost a slumberous night. I hardly slept one bit all night. Nettie Gilman and her sister Mary were on the boat. Miss Dorman got off at seven o'clock. Gma and I retired early.

Jun 18 We were called at 12 o'clock to prepare to get off the boat. We arrived at Aunt Nancy's at 12:30. Were very tired and sleepy We retired to get a little rest before was day. We did not get up very early. Lizzie Bear(Bare) came over to call early this morning. I went with her to the P.O. and other places over town. Wrote Mama, Rose, and C. Trude Bear(Bare) came in this evening. Met several of my cousins today. Took a walk this evening. Retired early.

Jun 19 Didn't get up until breakfast was ready. Felt very tired and sleepy. We were invited to spend the day at Aunt Mary Bear's. Had a real nice time. But felt a little lonely for a while. Took a walk over to the P.O. No mail for us. I was disappointed. I thought would get a letter from home. I think they might for they know I will get homesick if I don't get letters from there some times. Aunt Nancy was worse today than she has been since we came. I am afraid she will lose her mind entirely. Am going to retire early for am very tired and sleepy. I do not feel as well as I did before left home. Went to the graveyard where my Great-great-grandmother was buried. I gathered some flowers to remember the place. Came home. Retired early.

Jun 20 Grandma got up very early this morning We were up long before breakfast. I wrote a long letter to Marnie. Will have to go over to the office and mail it soon. Am trying to read *East Lymme*. It is a splendid book. Today is the first time it has caused me to shed tears. Finished *East Lymme* today. Went with Gma and

Aunt Nancy over in town. Dressed for the first time in a thin dress since left home this P.M. Dressed this evening to go over in town with Leida but it rained too hard to go out. Am going to bed early.

Jun 21 Got up early. Dressed for breakfast and after which dressed in blue silk to go to class meeting. Charley Oneill's little girl came up today for dinner. Went over to Aunt Mary's. Took tea there. Intended to have gone to S.S. and C but it was raining too hard to go to S.S. and had such a fearful headache didn't feel like going to C so came home. Went to bed as soon as could get my clothes off. I feel a little homesick today. I think if C does not write today he will be real mean. I don't think he is treating me one bit right. He knows that I am away up here and I think he might write a good long letter. He could write some if his arm does pain him.

Jun 22 Felt very weak and bad. I wish I could go home this morning. I am afraid I will have a severe sick spell before I ever get strong again. Sewed nearly all day on Gma's dress. Felt better this evening. Took a walk with Leida away up the river road. Came home late. Met Leida's sister.

Jun 23 Feel better this morning. Wrote to Ema and a postal to C. I bet he will be good and fooled when he gets it for I never wrote anything on it that he could tell whom it was from. Went over to Will Bear's for dinner had just a splendid dinner and a good time. Came back to Leida's for tea. Had a good supper. Helped her to make ice cream. Just as was finishing our supper, Trude came over and wanted me to go buggy riding with her and Sal. I went, of course. We went up to Buckhill Bottom, where Gma used to live. It is a very fine land up there. Enjoyed the trip splendid. Stopped at Allie's when we came home. Was so disappointed because did not get a letter from home. I just think they treat me real mean. If C does not write to me before I go home, I shall be very careful when I go home about writing to him. He has as much time to write as I have and is as able to do it too. The only excuse I can find for him is that he is home now and doesn't care who is away. I think he is just as mean as he can be about writing.

Jun 24 Leida and I intended to have gone down to Sardis today. But Grandma and Aunt Nancy went. Leida and I had a real nice time here. Took a walk this evening. Went to bed early. Went to Prayer Meeting. Not many there, not as many as there are at our little church. Did not get any letters today. I think it is real mean that some of them do not write.

Jun 15 Got up early. Finished up what braid I had. Wrote a letter home. Went over to the P.O. to mail it and get some more braid. Leida and I took quite a walk today. We went out over the hills. We walked about four miles over hills. We were so very tired when we came in. Took a buggy ride with Trude and Harry. We went down through Texas. Came home. Dressed for Miss Strain,but she did not come so L and I took a walk over in town. Grandma, Aunt Nancy, and Sis came home this P.M. Dressed in my white for the first time this P.M.

Jun 26 Felt almost too bad to crawl out but managed to get up in time for breakfast. Just as we were eating, Trude came over to tell us that Harry would go with us today to see them making cheese. Leida, Fannie, Sis, Harry, and myself went. We had an express without any springs. It was a little rough going but we enjoyed it ever so much.

The place we stopped at to see the cheese was a little two-room log hut. Here we found a Dutchman who couldn't scarcely understand English. The kettle that he boiled the milk in had a diameter of about 8 ft. The cheese that was in the press weighed from 1.5 to 1.6. He took us down in his cellar where there were

100 cheese of the same weight as the one upstairs. We purchased a little but it was not very good. It was just twelve o'clock when we were coming down off the high hill.

I was so very tired that went to my room immediately after reaching the house. Leida came in and brought me three letters from home. One from C. He is going back to Col. It made me homesick when I read his letter. I wish I could go home today. Wrote to C and Mary this P.M. Took a walk over in town. Went through Beuson's house.

Jun 27 I was so sore that did not feel like moving. Trude came over for me to go picknicking, but I told her I could not go for was too tired to go anywhere. Went over to Aunt Mary's for tea. Had a real nice time.

Jun 28 Had a severe spell of headache. Stayed in bed most of the day. Had something like a chill this morning. The two misses Strauss and Allie called this evening. I was in bed but got up and dressed for them. Enjoyed their call real well.

Jun 29 Feel some better this morning than did yesterday. Worked on the collar for Fannie all morning. Packed our things. Went over to Aunt Mary's to tell them "Good Bye". No one there but Aunt and Trude. We went over to the river early expecting the boat. She didn't come until late. Got to Matamoras before dark. Uncle met us at the river. Had a real pleasant trip on the boat. We are going to retire early.

Jun 30 It was late when we got up. Uncle went with us to look at the lower end of town. Saw the place where Gma first lived after she was married. The old well still was there but covered up. Saw where the old graveyard used to be. This P.M. we went in the upper part of town. It is a real pretty town considering its size. Called twice to see Jim Riggs' folks. Aunt Nancy seems so much better today. I am real lonesome. I wish we could go home today. The *Emma Graham* will not go down at all. We will have to take the *Chancello*r and only go to G. Then go from there on the little boat.

Jul 1 After almost a sleepless night I got up real early. I couldn't sleep hardly one bit all night. I want to go home. We, Grandma, Aunt Nancy, Aunt Betsy, Uncle H. and myself and the man who rowed us down in the skiff to Uncle Squire's got there about ten o'clock. It was a little rough on the water yet nevertheless I enjoyed the ride real well. Had a real pleasant day.

Jul 2 We went to Frank Riggs's for dinner. Had just a splendid time. His wife is so nice I liked her so much. Aunt N does not feel so well today. Am very tired. Will go to bed early. Never saw any thing of any importance but the history of my Great-great-grand-father. I wish I had a talent for writing. I would write a history.

Jul 3 I did not sleep well all night. We came down to Scott Riggs's for dinner and to wait for the boat. The boat never came until almost twelve o'clock. Had a very pleasant time. They have a lovely tree in their yard. I wish we could have one as nice at home.

Jul 4 We were just at Parkersburg when I got up. From the river it does not present a very lovely town. They say when you get out in town it is a real nice place. I hardly closed my eyes overnight. The boat was so full that we had just a little single room which was a very uncomfortable room for three to stay in. I thought my head would burst in the night. This morning I got up. I felt so bad couldn't hardly sit up so just had a cup of tea and went to bed staying until about ten o'clock. My head felt better so got dressed in my blue silk and went out in the cabin.

After Lizzie's trip upriver with her grandmother, she came home to life on the farm and assumed her duties there. Life for women revolved around cooking, sewing, doing laundry, letter writing, church activities, and entertaining. Notice the laundry was always done on Monday, followed by Tuesday's ironing. The rest of the week was routine as well. Short, clipped comments reflect boring days. November 1-14 seems to be as gray as the weather. Sunday always had reference to SS (Sunday School and C(church). References to "the burg" are probably to a nearby village south of the farm, Chambersburg, now Eureka. When Marnie, Lizzie's best friend, was married right out of high school, Lizzie disapproved and was very lonely without her companionship. Her wedding day was the second worst day of Lizzie's life so far. The Victorian melodramatic words paint their own picture.

◆   ◆   ◆

Routines on the Farm

Wed Jul 6 Got up early. Helped get dinner. Received a note from W. He is so sorry for his actions Saturday towards me. Feel very tired. But Marnie came along and wanted me to go to burg with her. I went. Dressed in my wrapper.

Thu Jul 9 Rose went to town. Made a dress for Aunt Nancy but sewing the buttons on. Had a little rain this evening.

Fri Jul 10 Helped with the work. Helped Rose to make her dress. Wrote to C.

Sat Jul 11 Had a great deal to do in getting the things ready for Quarterly meeting. Three or four here for dinner. Ida and Ena Gilman came down this evening. They are going to stay all night. Went to church this evening. A great many here.

Sun Jul 12 Helped get the work all done up so could go to church but just as I was almost ready, Aunt N would not go so I said I would stay at home with her. Got dinner almost ready when they came home. A great many here for dinner. Am very tired. I went to C this P.M. Wrote two letters this evening.

Mon Jul 14 Helped iron. Picked cherries. Teased Jim H. Got a letter from H.G.

Tue Jul 15 Sewed some. All the folks are gone today. Got a letter from Ena.

Wed Jul 21 Helped with work. Was greatly disappointed because did not get a letter.

Thu Jul 22 Had thrashers. It was so warm, couldn't hardly stand it.

Fri Jul 23 Had thrashers until noon when it commenced to rain. They all went home. Went to the burg. Got a letter from C. and mailed one to him. It rained hard this P.M. C's letter was so good.

Jul 24 Marnie and I went up to Aunt Colina's. She wasn't at home so went over to Aunt Mat. She was not at home so we went down to Rose William's for dinner and then went back to Aunt C. for supper. Had a real nice time. Came down in time for the baptizing. There were five immersed.

Jul 25 Helped with the work. After dinner went out to the picknick on the hill. A good many there. Clara G was jealous of me but I didn't care. I had some fun. Came home and put up some fruit. Got another letter from C. He feels so bad because I was so disappointed.

Sun Jul 26 Went to church and S.S. Several here for dinner. Was very tired but wrote to C.

Mon Jul 27 Had enormous big washing but it commenced to rain and did not get to put out all the clothes. Am very tired.

Tue Jul 28 Rose and I put out the clothes and ironed nearly all day

Wed Jul 19 Rose went to town. Had thrashers here again for dinner and supper. Finished "Barriers Burned Away" by EP Roe. It is splendid. It gave a good description of the Chicago Fire of 1876.

Thu Jul 30 They got through thrashing before they came to dinner. Marnie and I went up to Aunt Mattie's for supper. Had a splendid time.

Fri Jul 31 Marnie and I went to town. Stopped a few minutes at Mrs. Eckers. Got home a little after dinner. Emma Bay, Dr. Rathburn and wife, and Marnie here for supper. Got another letter from C. I think next time I will not be so hasty in writing.

Sat Aug 1 Helped with the work. Papa paid all the hands off today. I am very glad of it too. Went out to the picknick on the hill about ten o'clock. A great many there.

Tended to lemonade stand until Edd went and found someone to take my place and made me go with him to the swing where we had a splendid swing.

Ben Switzer, Jessie Hutsmiller and Miss Vanden came home with me for supper. Jessie and George were here when we got home. Henry Ida and Edith Gilman came down. I treated H real mean. We went over to Marnie's to go down to the river to take a skiff ride, but the skiff was not clean enough to take a ride in. Came home from the hill with Ben. He seemed like he did not like it at all. We made ice cream after. Came home at ten o'clock. Henry, Ida and Marnie, Jessie and George stayed all night

Aug 2 Henry and Jim talked almost all night last night. I couldn't sleep. Got up with a terrible headache H wanted me to go to the burg but I wouldn't. This P.M. he wanted me to take a buggy ride. Would not. I know I treat him mean but I cannot help it. Several here for dinner. Am very tired and sleepy. Wrote some to C.

Aug 3 Helped with the work. It rained so couldn't put out all the clothes.

Aug 4 Got up. Helped put out the clothes. When we got that done felt so bad had to go to bed. Felt too bad to sit up until late this P.M. Marnie was over today. I hate so bad to think of her getting married.

Aug 7 Marnie wanted me to come up to town and go up to Ena S. but it is raining too hard. Helped sew on the comfort for the children made from their mother's dresses. Poor dear sister. If only she could have stayed with us a little longer. My poor heart longs for her. It seems as though it will break.

Aug 8 Helped with the work. Mary, Rose, and Jim went to Cheshire. Some went to Clipper Mill. I had supper to get and wash dishes all alone. Am very tired. Am going to bed early.

Aug 11 I have been feel very sad all day for today is the last day I will have my own schoolmate. Marnie, Ada, and I went to the woods after ferns and moss to fix up some things for tomorrow. I only wish Marnie would not get married so soon. It seems to me that I cannot bear to think of it. I feel as though I would as most soon see her cold in death than marry that man. She will never be the same to me like she was before she chose someone to take my place. Oh! I have nothing to live for now. I would be willing to leave this life for the one that is to come.

Aug 12 Of all the days in my short life this is next to the saddest. I have had to take my cries in solitary of my own room. Marnie has been over several times. I dressed early and went over. M was not dressed. Met Mr. E's brother. I felt so embarrassed to think I would have to stand up with them with him. But I managed to do it without fainting. M looked real well but Mr. E did not look any more like a groom than Jim. His shoes were just awful. I was really ashamed of them. Everything went off real well. I was so afraid it would look awful. They got a great many presents. Several came to "bell" them but did not stay long.

Aug 13 Got up at two o'clock to go for the five o'clock train to go out to Mrs. Ewing's. M and Mr. E went in the single buggy. Ada, Ben, Ewing, Jim C., Jim R., and myself in the carriage. Did not get our breakfast until after we got there. Ewing met us at the station after supper. Mr. E came over to take us back to the station. Enjoyed ourselves real well but all of us was rather stupid and sleepy. All but Ben took a nap before dinner. Arrived at G 9:15. Came down home. Henry came out to the buggy to speak to us.

Aug 14 Did not get up until real late. Took Marnie's "Bible" down for Mr. Crooks to fill out the marriage certificate. Helped sew nearly all day. Feel somewhat tired all day. Wrote to C.

Aug 15 Wrote more to C. Wanted to go to town but couldn't. Helped with work. Went over to Marnie's. They hadn't been home but a short time. Went over to Claver to the social. Had a tolerable nice time. Came home early.

Aug 16 Went to S.S. There wasn't any church. Mr. E and Marnie, W, Auntie Rose, Reece, and Mattie here for dinner. This will be the last time poor Marnie will get to eat here for some time. I feel terrible bad. Finished a letter of thirty pages to C.

Aug 17 Helped do the work. M came over this P.M. to have her hair combed for the last time. I wish I was dead or could go away and never come back again.

Aug 18 I felt like my life was nearly at the last flow of the ebbing tide where the boat carried all that I have cared for from my youth from sight. I couldn't keep from crying. Oh! My heart is breaking I don't see how I can ever stand it. I long just once more to live over a few more happy months. Marnie has gone forever from me it seems. I wish she had never seen that man.

Aug 19 Yesterday was my birthday but I forgot all about it until today. Helped with the work. Received a long letter from C. What am I going to do. Trust I say "yes". Oh! that I only knew what to do. I long to do what is right but I am afraid I can never do it. Clara came over this evening.

Aug 22 Helped with work. Made some plum butter. Rose and Ed went out to Jessie's. Am awful tired and sleepy. Am going to bed early. I wish Marnie was here.

Aug 25 Went to ironing as soon as ate my breakfast. About nine o'clock looked out and saw a whole wagon load of folks coming. It was five of Mrs. Taylor's. Got through ironing while they were eating dinner. Cousin Roe H.'s two children here also for dinner. They went home soon after dinner but the others stayed for tea. Got a letter from M. Was so glad to hear from her. Was just going to bed when heard the boat whistling for the landing. Rookh and her cousin Ena Holloway came. I don't know what I will do. Am awful tired.

Aug 26 Got up early. Cleaned up part of the rooms. Fixed breakfast for the company while they were getting dressed for town. Went out to Jessie's for dinner. We came back by the way of Mr. Gilman's farm. Rookh thought she had found a horse that would suit her. She got on it and rode it in town. We, all but Eva, stayed at Mr. G's for tea. Rookh rode all the way home on her horse. Company for tea. Mrs. Booton, S, and Keller.

Aug 27 We didn't do much of anything only run around after a horse. Went to Aunt Sallie's for dinner. Rookh didn't feel well all day. Clara came over this evening.

Aug 29 Helped with the work. Made some grape jelly. Rose went down to Grandma's to stay the night.

Aug 30

Oct 25 You darling old book! How could I be so neglectful as to leave you so long! Nothing of so great importance has happened since I last wrote. I have once more acted very mean to C. I long for Thursday. Last Wednesday Grandma, Aunt Sue, Rookh, Mama and myself took dinner at Mr. Willie Thorinlays. Had a delightful time. I guess I will write a little to C today if I never send it. I feel very lonely today. I only wish I knew a few things. How I long to see Marnie. Why don't she come to see me? If she doesn't soon come I will surely die. I must see her.

Oct 26 Felt very lonely and bad all day. This P.M. heard a boat coming. Looked out and beheld the darling old girl coming home. I was so glad. Couldn't scarcely wait until I had seen her. Got a very brief letter from C. I think he misjudges me greatly.

Oct 27 Helped iron all forenoon. Marnie came over this evening for a while. She has changed wonderfully since she was married.

Nov 1 When I got up found that it had great appearance of rain. It rained so we did not go to church. Went over to Will's this P.M.

Nov 2 Still raining. H and A went home this morning. Helped with the work.

Nov 3 Helped with the work.

Nov 4 Did as usual. Marnie and Rose went to town. Rose got my cloak.

Nov 5 Made apple butter.

Nov 6 Rained all day.

Nov 7 Helped with the work. Marnie came home this evening.

Nov 5 Made apple butter.

Nov 6 Rained all day.

Nov 7 Helped with the work. Marnie came home this evening.

Nov 10 Helped with the work.

Nov 12 Did as usual. Nothing.

Nov 13 Marnie started for home today. I hated to see her go so bad. Worked with the knitting machine.

Nov 14 Didn't do much of anything.

In the fall, farmers took their bounty to New Orleans by boat. The Riggs family, along with others, seem to have leased a boat. Lizzie's Uncle Amos and Jim, a cousin or a brother, were shepherding the produce on the long trip. Apparently, several boats from the area traveled together in a kind of flotilla. Lizzie and a friend, perhaps a cousin, Clara, went along in November. Their duties were much what they were at home: cooking, cleaning, washing, ironing. Each day was a new sight for Lizzie. She doesn't chafe nearly as much as she had earlier in the summer about the lack of mail from home. Although she is tired much of the time and still suffers headaches, she manages her responsibilities and seems to have a good time when they are docked. Nearly every stop she at least goes "up on the bank" and often makes it all the way into town where going to the Post Office is an event. The experience must have matured her. The captain and her relatives serve as suitable chaperones, but she manages to "keep company" with quite a number of fellows in this man's world of the river. Her account of the trip supplies an itinerary down the Ohio and Mississippi complete with anecdotes and descriptions from the towns along the way.

◆   ◆   ◆

Adventure South

Nov 17 Packed my trunk to go this evening. Had lots to do. Clara came over to stay until the boat came. Went to bed early.

Nov 18 About 11 o'clock last night we heard a fearful cry, "There's the boat!" That was enough. We bounced out of bed in a hurry, dressed, and had to run all the way to the river. This morning it was rainy when we got up. We found a very dirty house which took all forenoon to get cleaned out. We found no ladies on board, but C and I. Papa came down to Ashland with me and hated to see him leave. Wrote a postal to Marnie at Portsmouth which space we passed just at twilight. C and I found our next-door neighbor to be Guss Martindale. Got acquainted with the Cap and _____.

Nov 19 When we got up, we found us near Maysville. When we got to Ripley about 9 o'clock one of our distant relatives came on board, Jacob Riggs. Ripley is a very nice place. Passed Grant's old home at Point Pleasant, O. We could see the place but not the house where he was born. Mr. Riggs got off at Higginsport about eleven o'clock. Augusta is the most beautiful town. New Richmond was a lovely place. The boat ceased running about 9 o'clock P.M., six miles above Cinc. Had callers this P.M., pilot and _____.

Nov 20 We are likely to stay here most of the day. Several of the boys went down to the city today. Jim R, Clara, Sylvia, and myself went down this P.M. Stayed until the boat came down which was about three o'clock. We went out in the city as far as the P.O. C and I went up in the pilot house. Pilot came down this evening. Were passing Lawrenceburg at 9 o'clock.

Nov 21 Passed Harrison, last resting place during the night. It was just above the city of Madison. It was a lovely town. Wrote home this P.M. Baked bread and scrubbed. Clara sick the A.M. I have such a fearful headache cannot rest at all. Landed at Jeffersonville for the night. Today is the first pretty day we have had since we left home.

Nov 22 Raining this morning. Feel some better this morning but do not feel very well. C and I went over to Sydna for dinner. This A.M. C and I went to the top of the hill in the mud and rain to say we had been in Jeffersonville, Ind. If I felt well, I would go out in town. This P.M. Jim R., C, Jim C., and myself went out to the P.O. J is a lovely town when you once get down to the town. Saw a levee for the first time. Mr. Haptonstall came in this evening and stayed until late. I like him ever so much. He is very congenial. We will stay here until morning. I feel much better this morning.

Nov 23 Came down to Louisville. Landed near the city wharf. C, Uncle Amos, Will G, and I went out in town. I think this about as pretty a city as I ever saw. They have such lovely dwelling houses. Mr. H here a greater portion of the forenoon. Mr.C came down this P.M. He took C and I to see them let the boats through the locks and to see the falls (which are not very much of a sight from where we stood.) It did not inspire me with the grandeur that I expected. Saw Portland in the far distance. The Falls have a fall of about 50 ft. in 5 miles. Mr. C feels badly from the way he has acted. Could not get through the locks until after night. Captain Merle and Mr. H were down this evening.

Nov 24 I did not sleep scarcely any all night. I was terrible sick. Feel too weak this morning to move. We were scarcely out of sight of Louisville this morning. Jim helped me wash this A.M. While we were at dinner, while gazing from our window, we saw the water gushing from a solid rock of the cliff about 200 ft. high. It called to mind a passage of scripture in the bible where Moses smote the rock. C. Washed this P.M. I ironed.

Nov 25 I feel terrible mean today Do not feel sick or well. Sylvia was sick, and we concluded we would have the dinner tomorrow so sent an invitation to the pilot and Mr. C. They accepted. This morning the sun was just coming above the horizon when we beheld Cloverport, Ind. At Carrolton, Ky. there was an island called Rock Island. It used to be the terror of steamboat men. Passed some lovely scenery today. Mr. A. down. C and I made complete _____ with our cakes.

Nov 26 Did not sleep very well all night. Our dinner was real nice. Just as we were getting ready for dinner, Jim R went out and killed a wild goose. I had a terrible time trying to get it dressed. This P.M. Mr. H, J.R., C. and I went out to Mt. Vernon, Ind. There we learned that our Vice President (Thomas A. Hendricks, Vice-President in Grover Cleveland's first administration.) had departed this life last night at 6 P.M. Jim took C and I up in the pilot house this P.M. I read a great deal this evening. I have had lots of fun today. I wonder what they are doing at home.

Nov 27 This morning found us tied up to the bank just above and opposite Caseyville, Ky. After breakfast C and I went out in the woods. Found some lovely ferns and other flowers. Mr. H. brought in a large bouquet this morning to us from the woods. The boat layed up for coal until 1 P.M. Jim R, J,C, Ed, C and I all went out in a skiff to Canen Rock. Just before we came to the cave, there was the lovliest scenery I have seen since we left home. There was an abrupt cliff of rock about 100 ft. high. Above this cliff could be seen the evergreen cedar. It was a grand picture to the eye of an artist. When we entered the Cave, it impressed me with solemnity. I should judge on entering the cave that it was about 50 ft. high and 100 ft wide, while back 75 ft to 100 was about 20 ft wide and ten ft. in height. In the center of the cave was an opening into which, as tradition has it,"pirates" lived. They would kill the rivermen and dispose their property. In this opening there is a large room. Two of the boys went through the opening. They brought forth some lovely rock which had never seen daylight after their formation. We all enjoyed our ride. We ate dinner with Sylvia today. Mr. C is very sulky toward us today. Mr. H was down when we came home.

Nov 28 Felt bad but managed to keep up until after dinner. Went to bed. Got to Cairo about dark. Felt too bad to go out. Clara and Jim went. Edd stayed with me.Will brought me some oranges. They were real nice. Owen Drummond called on us this evening. Mr. H in for a few minutes.

Nov 29 Felt some better this morning. We had S.S. this P.M. Went out in Missouri for some stones. Almost killed myself laughing at Sydna. He tore his pants on the barbed wire fence. Mr. H went out in Tenn. with me this P.M. Feel pretty good this morning.

Nov 30 C, Jim and I washed. C and I ironed. Nothing of special interest today. Am very tired. Mr. H down.

Dec 1 How time is flying! Everything going on nicely. Landed near Fort Pillow, Tenn. Went out on the bank. Mr. H came in this evening. Got some lovely rock at Fort Pillow.

Dec 2 Commenced my stocking today. Dressed for the first time in anything but my everyday clothes. Went out boating with the boys. Met Mr. Lower this P.M. Had letter from Rose, the first one from home. Went out in Memphis, Tenn. with Mr. H. M is a real pretty town, much nicer than I had expected. Enjoyed the trip splendid.

Dec 3 Didn't sleep scarcely any all night. Feel terrible bad all forenoon. Called on our new neighbors. For the first time was in a sail boat. They have things fixed up real nice in it. Mr. H here nearly all P.M. I quarreled with him this evening for fun though. Went out on top of the bank when the boat landed for the night.

Dec 4 Tied up early in the evening for the night. Had quite a _____ this evening. The young men from the sail boat gave it to us. Mr. H down. Had a splendid time.

Dec 5 I feel terrible bad. Am afraid I'm going to have a sick spell today. Tied up early for the night. Mr. H down this evening.

Dec 6 Never got up until late. Ed and Will went down to Red River this morning. Was up to the pilot house. Mr. Thompson came up while we were there. I like him real well. Mr. H down this evening. Landed at Arkansas City tonight. Feel terrible blue and sick this evening.

Dec 7 We were still tied up to the bank until noon. Washed, ironed. Had picture of the boats this P.M. They think they will be real good. Went out on the banks this evening. Ed and Will went to Greenville this P.M.

Dec 8 The wind was blowing terrible this morning. Had to tie up after a run of two miles. Clara, Jim, and I went out. Took a walk of 3 miles for pecans. Was so very tired when got back to the boat. Mr. H brought Mr. T in this evening. Had some lovely music. They stayed until very late. Never saw only two miles run today.

Dec 9 Felt terrible bad this morning. Did not feel one bit like getting dinner for company. Mr. H, Mr. T, and Captain Caphan here for dinner. Ed came to us at noon. Clara, Edd, and I went out in Greenville this P.M. Had just lots of fun. Clara and I fell down in the skiff coming home. Mr. H down. All enjoyed their dinner.

Dec 10 Found we were on our way this morning. Knit nearly all day. Skinned a bird that Mr. H killed yesterday. Mr. H down for supper. Landed early for the night. Painted some this P.M. The second painting I ever done in my life.

Dec 11 We were slowly wending our way down the Miss. River. Went up in the pilot house for the last time on this trip. Got the pictures of the fleet today. UncleAmos had an attack of heart trouble. Ed had severe spell of head ache this evening. Mr. H here for a few minutes. Mr. T gave us a sernaid this evening on the organet. He stayed until late. Got letter from Marnie. Clara and I will stop at Vicksburgh tomorrow. We landed at Kings Point for the night. Will met us here this evening.

Dec 12 Early this morning commenced to pack our things to leave the boat. Dressed in a hurry. Jim came out in the skiff after us. I hated to leave Ed feeling bad, but he is much better this morning. The boys came over to bid us farewell. We got out to Mr. Kirk's about three o'clock this P.M. They were all so glad to see us. Have a severe headache. Will retire early. Got three letters.

Dec 13 I feel better this morning. Went to the M.E.(Methodist) S.S. and C this morning. This P.M. to the Episcopalian. This evening to Baptist. Enjoyed the sermons very much. Several called on us today.

Dec 14 Feel real well this morning. Ida went with C and I to the public school building. The principal was so kind to us. This P.M. we walked out to the National Cemetery. That is just a grand place. There are 16600 soldiers buried there. Have two fountains on the grounds. The government keeps it fixed up nicely. Am very tired. Several ladies called on us today. Got letter from Rose and Ernie.

Dec 15 Didn't feel very well today. C and I took quite a walk this morning. Ida, C, and I walked down to the flat boat this P.M. Felt terrible tired and sick when I got home. Got letter from C. Had a taffy pulling this evening.

Dec 16 Felt terrible stiff and sore. Ida and I went out in town twice. This evening Mrs. Rand, Ida, Clara, and I went to call of Miss Woodyard. Then we went to stay all night with Miss Taylor. Enjoyed the evening.

Dec 20 Woke up, got up, fixed our things so we can send them down by Jim this P.M. Ida, Clara, and I went to the Catholic Church this morning. Ida and I took a walk before dinner. They had the nicest dinner for us today. This P.M. Ida, Clara, L, and I walked out to the City Cemetery. It made me feel awful bad to see everything going to ruin. It looked like a desert. Jim was here when we got home. He looked real bad. Ida, Mrs Trimble, and I went to the Baptist church this evening. There was a young lady immersed. I feel very lonely and bad.

Dec 21 I awoke very early. Got up and dressed to leave. After breakfast Clara, Kirk, and myself walked down to the boat. Found them all very busy. C and I got dinner. I tended to Sydra's bread. Will said he hated to have us leave. He asked me a few necessary questions. I feel sorry to see them working as hard as they are. The boat came in about four o'clock. Will took us down to the boat. Instead of the *Ed Richardson* we took the Pan's *The Brown*. Found Mrs. Moore and her children on board. I have terrible sore throat—am going to retire early.

Dec 22 Didn't get up very early. My throat is not much better. Found several nice passengers aboard but none I cared to associate with. Used up all my thread so haven't anything to do but read until Clara gets through with my needles. Commenced *Children of Abbey*. Don't like it very much. Nothing of any interest.

Dec 23 This morning found us still winding our way down the Miss. Got to Natchez just before noon. The boat stayed here quite awhile but I didn't feel like going out.

Dec 24 Found ourselves tied up to the bank on account of fog. My throat is still sore. We started around eight o'clock. I watched for the *Katie* until noon. Then after dinner I felt so bad I laid down. She met us about 2 o'clock. I did not get to see her. I feel so disappointed because no one came for us.

Dec 25 Another year has rolled by. One more year for Christ. The sun came up in all its beauty to celebrate the birth of our dear Savior. But alas! For me this doesn't seem one bit like Christmas. Didn't receive anything but candy. Never gave anyone anything but Jim. Left him a shaving mug. Jim Clark came up to the boat for us.

Came down to the boat. Then Jim took us out to see a steam ship and up in town. Saw Jackson's Square. It is a real pretty place.

Dec 26 Didn't feel well enough to go around so stayed home and worked all day.

Dec 27 Finished *The Children of the Abbey* a little after ten o'clock. Got up late. Ed, Uncle Amos went with Clara and I out in town after dinner. Uncle A left us. Then Ed took us to Lake Pontchatrain on the train. This lake is of considerable size. We couldn't see over it. We only went to the west end. It was a beautiful place. Several bath houses, large hotel, and a puzzle made of evergreen. Here we wandered around for some time before we could find our way out. In the center of the puzzle is a cave made from rock. We passed through this and went the entire way through the puzzle. After we had come out, several others were in there. It was real funny to see them trying to get out. Coming home we stopped at the cemetery. Here instead of having the graves made down in the ground, they build vaults. Some are made of brick cemented over. Those of stone in the greater part are made of granite and marble. There were some magnificent vaults. It always makes me feel sad to think how many bright hopes lay hidden there. The grounds have not been kept up quite as nice as those at the National Cemetery. But everything was real nice. Received letter from Eva and note from L—wrote to D. I am afraid it will hurt his feelings but cannot help it.

Dec 28 Got up real early. Jim and Clara and I started to the Exposition. On entering the grounds it inspired me. In the main building I was greatly disappointed. I expected to find a great many more things and nicer. From the Main building we went south to the Government building. Here we found a great many nice things. Each state was arranged to represent the custom of living among the people. Thought that Colorado was the nicest representation. There was a little house made of the different kinds of minerals. Not far from the house was a farm with every thing fixed just like you would find on a farm. Near the farm was a small lake with sailboats floating over its surface.

From the Government building we went to the Art Gallery. Here were a great many magnificent pictures. From here we entered the Horticultural Hall by ascending and descending a bridge.

Saw bananas here, green and then blossoms. Cactus. They were about 12 ft. high and 1 ½ ft through. There were a great many foreign plants there.

We stayed on the grounds until after three. Started for home. Was so tired couldn't scarcely move when got home.

Dec 29 Got up but not refreshed by any means. Went to washing as soon as got through breakfast. Had to hurry like anything to get through in time to get dinner. Can scarcely move am so tired. I had a big washing. Am going to bed early.

Dec. 30 I got up. Did not feel one bit well. My limbs are as stiff as an old government mule. Washed out my flannels this morning. Then commenced to iron. I got all out of whack for only had one iron and had to wait so much that never got through until after three o'clock. Am very tired. Am going to bed early.

Dec 31 After we got the work done up, went out in town wandered nearly all over the town. Came home just before dinnertime and had to get dinner. Felt all out of humor for was so very tired did not want to do any thing. This P.M. Jim and Clara and I went down to the mint. We were only gone a few moments. They were not in "blast" so we couldn't see very much. Saw where they were hauling the money away. There was $25,000.00 on one load.

There was 10,000 in each sack. Our guide did not show us around so very much.

Another year is gone with it many of my bright hopes have fled. Oh! What have I done to the advancement of Christ cause during this year? Have I been the cause of any soul being born again?

I hope during the coming year I may make some improvements on my past life. I want to live a closer walk with my Savior. I want to make more people happy. I guess I will retire soon and see if cannot begin fresh with the New Year. Good Bye, dear old book. Many a sad _____ lay buried upon your pages. Many a happy one also remains.

◆   ◆   ◆

At the back of Lizzie's journal, she documents her frugal spending.

Trip to New Orleans

Stamp	.25
Dimmoned Dye	.10
Doll Baby	.25
Stamps	.25
Shaving Mug for Jim	.45
Day book	.05
Thread	.10
Wash rag	.05
Handkerchiefs	1.05
Car fare	.05
Fare to Ponchatrain	.20

To Exposition/car fare	.65
Passage on Paris E.Brown	8.00
Hair cut	.25
Car fare	.10
Mug for Ed	.25
Collars	<u>.15</u>
	13.95
	<u>21.</u>
	34.95

1885
Spent

Jan 5	Fare on Telegraph	.50
Jan 5	Hair Cut	.25
Jan 5	Buttons for Dress	.10
Jan 5	Rent	1.25
Jan 5	Paid Marnie	.25
Jan 7	Gave to Church	.03
Jan 7	Stamps	.10
Jan 9	Canton flannel	.84
Jan 11	Missionary money	.02
Jan 12	For the treasury	.30
Jan 12	Fare on boat	.35
Jan 12	For the Treasury	.30
Jan 12	Put away for Grandma	1.50
Jan 14	Paper	.10
Jan 14	Corset strings	.05

Jan 16	Passage on Boat	.15
Jan 19	Bought singing book	.25
Jan 21	Diary	.20
Jan 21	paper 10 and nest eggs 10	.20
Jan 19	For treasury	.30
Jan 23	Cough drops 5 and thread 5	.10
Jan 28	Dimond Dye 5 mucilage 10	.15
Jan 28	Gave to Sexton of ME Church	.05
Feb 3	Passage on boat 15 corset l.00	1.15
Feb 3	Rent	1.25
Feb 3	Treasury	.03
Feb 9	Passage	.35
Feb 9	Treasury	.20
Feb 17	Veil	.70
Feb 17	Paid Dr. Rathburn	.35
Feb 19	Had chain and pin fixed	.35
Feb 19	Fruits for cake	.93
Feb 28	Astronomy	1.40
M. 2	Rent	1.25
M. 2	Treasury	.10
M. 3	Gave Rose 50, Stamps 10	.60
M. 9	Books 40, 35, mucilage	.85
M. 9	Passage 35 treasury 10 5	.40
M 16	Stamps	.12
M 20	Passage	.35
M 23	Meadison for myself	.75
M 23	Trimming for cloths	.75
M. 24	pencil 5 treasury 30	.35

Ap 1	rent	1.67
" 2	buttons 10 for book for C	3.00
" 6	tablet 5 postal cards 5 trimming 20	.30
" 13	passage 35 treasury 10	.45

Trip to Bearsvilla (corrected to Baresvilla)

Passage on boat	$4.00
Feather edge braid	.60
Passage on Courier	.35
Supper	.15
Porter for our baggage	.10
From Matamoras to Uncle's	.25
Candy	.10
Passage home on Chancellor	3.10

APPENDIX B

Lizzie's Essay

L izzie's diary of her senior year at the Gallia Academy mentions over and over the essay that she delivered at her commencement. She left behind several essays on 5 x 7 sheets of striped tablet including this "American Parlor," but also "Niagara Falls," "Josiah Gilbert Holland," "Mark Twain," "Washington Irving," and "Joseph Addison." The essay on Twain does not mention either the stories of Tom or Huck, written in 1876 and 1884; the diary was written in 1885.

Whether any of these sample writings was "THE" essay she delivered after many rewrites from March until June, many practices, and much nervous tension, nevertheless, this Victorian version of the importance of the American parlor shows Lizzie's aspirations, Victorian style—both in writing and in decorating as well as Lizzie's gentle humor. It would have been my choice, as an English teacher, of all the essays for a public performance. The fresh viewpoint certainly would entertain the audience better than the rather dull lives of authors or geographical wonders. If it was "THE" essay, the draft here needed much more editing, but she worked on it for several months before her performance. I added some editing but leave some of her unusual punctuation for the reader to enjoy:

131

AMERICAN PARLOR
By
Lizzie C. Riggs

How many of us know what a real genuine American parlor is? Do we imagine it some fairy room, where only fairies dwell, or some large room where all sorts of people are employed with different kinds of occupation?

Doubtless you all have been in a real American parlor or have heard of them; where the walls are magnificently decorated with handsome painting and engravings of the most delicate tastes and styles: while the floor is covered with an elegant velvet carpet, soft covered sofas and chairs, while the curtains are of the finest lace. In fact, the very atmosphere of the room is that of grandeur. Many of the American Ladies have such parlors, but they keep them to admire themselves instead of having them for their friends to enjoy their beauty. They will keep the blinds closed and windows down to keep the room clean and save her the trouble of cleaning it, while she only opens it once or twice during the entire year to admit visitors or sunshine.

True, it is some trouble for a lady after she has given the last chair its relief of every particle of dust, to have a mischievous brother, without ceremony, to come stalking in the room with his heavy, muddy boots, and dancing from one corner of the room to the other, never thinking of the chairs and vases he knocks down, nor the quantity of mud he leaves on the carpet, yet he goes on to have some fun, as he expresses it. You might imagine hearing the noise, that there were twenty boys instead of one.

You may ask if we would have a parlor? Most assuredly we would, for what lady in the middle rank of society, and doing her work with the aid of only one servant would want visitors shown into the disordered sitting room, where the family clothing is being made on the tireless machine, and where five of "Dame Cornilia's Jewels", ranging between the ages of three and sixteen, though good and obedient will leave their books and blocks on any corner table, or anywhere it is convenient for them to leave them. It is not carelessness but thoughtlessness; it will save the Lady many an embarrassment by having a room, where she might receive her visitors without taking them in the disordered room.

Our American parlor should be a large cheerful room, with plenty of air and sunshine, and elegantly furnished with soft-cushioned chairs and sofas, beautiful and interesting pictures, a grand piano, opened free to all, interesting books by the best authors, velvet carpet, which will admit sunshine without losing any of its former beauty, and lace curtains which will resist the picture of Bridget's fingers, when they come in contact with the washboard, yet fine enough to throw a soft delicacy over every object in the room. And in the mammoth glass plate windows, should be found the snowy calla lily, the tea rose, the scarlet cactus, and the fragrant heliotrope breathing out its day of sweetness. Each member of the family should spend a part of each day in this room.

It is such a parlor as this that we would like for you all to have in your homes. Such a one has proved a haven of refuge, saved many a step, given calmness to the throbbing nerves, and has added many a peaceful rest to the weary.

The parlor can never be abolished while such sacred memoirs cluster around it. There in the long ago when the lighted lamp threw its rosy radiance over vases, pictures, and we held sweet communion with friends now separated from us by rivers and mountains of half a continent.

There, too, the majestic Christmas Tree, lighted with its hundred tiny, twinkling stars rose from the fairy gloom, while the happy children danced gleefully around it.

There the favorite daughter, a blushing bride, received her new name and gave her life into the keeping of another.

There lay the darling of the household, in her long, sweet sleep, with lilies clasped in her waxen hands. Ah, that room is holy; it is haunted by angel form, and in the twilight we have almost felt the brushing of their wings.

Appendix C

Edited Courtship Letters

◆

Berte Ingels to Lizzie Riggs
January 1889–September 1890

Reading these letters is like looking into a Victorian time capsule. From Berte's early note requesting permission to call to the last letter from Lizzie after their marriage, we get a glimpse into the times. Berte courts Lizzie with impassioned pleas and romantic language. Yet, his passion for her makes it impossible for him to visit as often as he or she would like. He finds it more bearable to stay away than to be near and not able to touch and hold her as he wants. He apologizes for his actions on some occasions.

Berte's personality comes through these letters. He is ever the romantic, unable to make decisions, but seems to idolize his Lizzie. Several times his explanations of his exploits seem to "protest too much". You can imagine Lizzie's state when she read them. He might have been in big trouble with his sweetheart.

The letter from Lebanon, Ohio, was written while Berte was enrolled in the Normal School there apparently for a spring or summer semester. Thivener, Ohio, was the home of Jessie Ingels, Berte's father. Thivener was probably no more than fifteen miles from the Raccoon Island farm of Lizzie's father, Jacob Riggs. Yet correspondence was necessary because work time was precious, travel was hard, and telephones were non-existent. Evidently, the mails went out several times a day. Post Offices in each community were busy and important places.

Berte tells Lizzie to burn his letters, yet they remain. She kept them in a wooden box for jellies, an appropriate place for sweet memories. Only one of her letters remains from this time period, written after their marriage but before they had set up housekeeping together.

Although I have edited Berte's letters to make them easier to read, the words remaining are his, if I have deciphered his handwriting correctly. I have occasionally deleted some sentences if they seem unrelated or repetitive. Meet Berton H. Ingels, Esquire.

Pleasant View,
Jan. 16, 1889

Miss Riggs:--

Will it be agreeable for me to call some evening? If so, please inform me at your earliest convenience.

Believe me to be your friend,

Berte Ingels

◆   ◆   ◆

Lebanon, Ohio
April 1, 1889

Miss Riggs:--

You need not look for me next Sunday, as you know perhaps that I am in Lebanon so you will not get your books in two weeks, but I will write home and have them sent home or down to Sallie's where you can get them sometime when you call. I will call again for them when I return about the middle of June. As Ada says, "That will be an excuse."

I came out too late for Ross and I to get a room together so I was left without a room-mate and had to go into a private family, but I am well pleased with my situation. The landlady is a very courteous and kind, pleasant and intelligent lady. Next week I will live as one of the family and that will be more like home. I haven't become very well acquainted yet, but I will soon become acquainted.

There isn't anything of interest in Lebanon except the school. The only improvement I see going on in the town is the erection of electric lights.

My studies are: Advanced Rhetoric or Harts American Literature, Latin, Philosophy, Debating, Authors of the Bible (a Sunday study) and vocal music.

I chose this paper because it is ruled better than my notepaper and as I am tired and sleepy I could not write upon unruled paper.

If there is anything of interest comes up about Clay (Township), please write and tell me.

Berte H. Ingels

◆   ◆   ◆

Thivener, Ohio
Sep 1889

Dear Friend:--

I will write to you this week so I can stand it to stay away for two weeks at least. I hope you will not object to me writing (just what I think) this time anyway. You can destroy my letter after you read it.

I know you think I am hard to understand for others have told me they can not understand me by my actions so I will be plain in my writing. Judging from your conversation you think I only want to call for pastime. It may be that that ought to be the case, nevertheless, I must say that I am too much in earnest to come for pastime. That would be flirtation, and I cannot be guilty of flirtation with you because you are more than worthy of me. I feel unworthy of your company, but I desire it nevertheless. Do you doubt my sincerity now- Let my confession this time be sufficient now and forever—

I feel unable to make you happy, but I am sure that your innocent character and childlike faith in God is a stimulation for me. In other words, you are a stimulant for me. I would be glad if you would stay at home just for the sake of your company, but as you know we must make sacrifices in order that we may succeed so I will be willing to make the sacrifice of seeing you go if it will be beneficial to you and if your health will not be endangered thereby. Of course, it is best not to stay in school when we feel that it does not agree with us, but it is better to return immediately to the farm—If you go at all now is the time. The best season of the year to study—but I believe that 6 months is enough school in one year, (i.e.) if we study very much.

Please answer favorably, I mean encouragingly, and excuse all mistakes and blots and scribbling.

As ever your friend,

Berte H. Ingels

All blots are kisses you know! You know! And this is a big one. (Blot appears on paper here.)

An envelope postmarked earlier than this was addressed to Lizzie C. Riggs at Box 391, Dallas, Texas. It was marked "Closed" and forwarded to Raccoon Island, Ohio. My guess is that Lizzie went to Texas to help her friend Marnie, who may have moved there. Perhaps she was having a baby or she was ill. I have no further clues. Lizzie was very close to Marnie and was quite upset when she married right out of high school.

◆   ◆   ◆

Thivener, Ohio
Jan 13, 189

Dear Friend:--

I haven't time to write much tonight, but I must write something since you have not heard from me for a month or so. I do not know why my letter did not reach you. I am very sorry that it is so for I certainly did not intend that you should be neglected.

I have been very busy for the last 3 wks. preparing for a Christmas entertainment, which I gave at my school. I had to study every night. We have had about 35 kids more or less to wait on for the last two weeks, and I have been taking lessons in painting for 2 or 3 nights so you see that I have plenty of excuses. Sufficient to say that I very much desire that you do not release me but have the confidence in my royalty(sic) to you that you please.

I do not know of any girl in the world who would suit me as well as you.

Come home as soon as possible for I am very anxious to see you. You certainly made a sacrifice in going off down there running the risk of your life. Of course, it was your love for Marnie that took you to her. I wish you thought as much of me as that. If you had, you might have stayed at home this winter.

Yet it may be all for the best. I will try to think so anyhow.

Well, as this is New Year, I am willing to forget the past and commence anew—

Please excuse all mistakes and scribbling in this letter.

I am in a place where I cannot get hold of a pen and ink. I will try to write a better letter in a few days. I tell you I would be glad to see you about now.

Write and tell me when you are coming home.

I hope you will be ready to start about the time this letter reaches you—

In great haste I remain as ever (yours forever)—

Berte H. Ingels.

◆   ◆   ◆

Thivener, Ohio
January 23, 189.

Dear Lizzie:--

I hoped to have seen you ere now, but fate says no for it has marked us for her own. I can't tell how long, but I do know that the "Grip", has fastened its clutches on the whole family. We are all down sick. It is certainly a pitiful sight to see the whole family sick at one time.

I certainly could appreciate your presence now I am sure, because I always get the blues when I have to stay indoors so long—

I hope you will allow me to make up for last time when I get better. I am trying to get well enough to come down Sunday and stay a wk or less.

If I am not able to be there Sunday, strike out over the hills to see me. Yes, that's the way to talk.

I think I will quit with teaching soon and withdraw from the profession forever—

School teaching is not my work—Everything seems to be drifting me towards the ministry, and I hope to be able to give it my whole attention from now on. It's hard to tell what may come between me and the goal for which I am striving, but I will trust Providence to guide me into the work for which I am destined.

If I cannot come down Sunday, write a great big long letter. I will come as soon as I do get better if it is right in the middle of the wk.

Tell Sallie that we are all sick. Our family and Herb also.

Yours forever & ever—

B.H. Ingels

Excuse pencil, again.

◆　　　◆　　　◆

Thivener, Ohio
Sun eve, 90.

Dear Lizzie:--

As the company has dispersed, it leaves me rather lonely this evening with no one to converse with but you and at a distance not exactly agreeable. I would rather be very near just now, but things can not always be just as we would wish. I wrote to you Friday and intended to go to the office Sat. and mail it, but I received your letter Fri evening and then I didn't think it necessary to make my trip to the office. I have been very busy this wk. and neglected to go down to Mrs. Serriere's after the mail Wednes—I had written to you that I would not come Sun. so it was alright that you didn't tell me to come Sun. It makes us feel bad for a day or so, and that won't do when you have so much on hand just now. So if you have any special reason that I should make a visit soon, then inform me soon and I will certainly obey and that willingly.

I told my sister-in-law our intentions, as I had an opportunity to do so today. She did not hesitate to say, "Yes, go ahead. I would not advise you to go on a circuit alone for you will need some friend to whom you can tell all your troubles, and receive sympathy and love in return. If she loves you, take her." I told her that my willingness was decided and the only question with either of us now is my health, sufficient to allow me to be successful on a circuit. The answer was, "I do not think she bothers herself about that very much. If she really loves you, she will take that risk and then do what she can to make you successful." If I am not successful, I believe the very cause of my failure will be in not believing that "All things are possible to him that believeth". I know my health is not very good, but my success depends upon my ability to "Trust." That's the greatest trouble. I cannot put my trust in God as I should. I must learn to trust him.

Emma says if you will be happy together, your happiness will be the means of improving your health. Now if that be so, I am sure to become strong, for I am very certain that I can not be mistaken in my love for you. That's true as steel. I am not dreaming now but there was a day or so I had to "pinch myself" to see if I was awake.

I am wide-awake now. Nothing but future time can tell whether we shall change our decision or not. I hope things may come out well. Emma says still another thing, "It is wrong not to get married," or at least one of her old fellows told her that.

I agree with him to a certain extent, for I think myself that every one ought to get married sometime in life if they have no cause for not doing so if it be convenient to do so. In our case, I fear it is not convenient for it may be that you will regret of ever having loved such an insignificant creature as I. My unworthiness worries me a great deal but as for me, you need not worry, for I am willing to take you for better or for <u>worse.</u>

Berte

◆   ◆   ◆

Thivener, O.
May, 1890

Dear Lizzie,

I expect to see you Sunday but I cannot wait until then to tell you how your letter surprised me. It was a great surprise. I congratulated myself for writing such a good letter, but your letter has caused me to think that I was greatly mistaken. Really, since I have come to think about what I wrote, it was ridiculous when I take the second thought of the sentence, "I didn't love you at the time you made your confession."

Now, candidly, that was not what I meant although what I meant to say was more than I will say again. You remember that I was feeling greatly depressed that evening and really I didn't have much sense that evening as is proven in the last letter I wrote. This is what I meant to say, "I was not altogether decided in my mind and heart that I loved you as you did me." I was not aware that girls are more affectionate than boys. I believe now that a woman's love is greater than a man's, don't you? Certainly, and now even if it were so that I didn't love you as tenderly as you did me, was it not alright for you to say you loved me. Believe me when I say that my heart was not so hard as not to have any love for you at that time, but my mistake was as I have said I thought I ought to love you as sincerely as you did me.

You know I am a slow creature to make up my mind, but I am very sure that it is made up now, and I feel that I must have your forgiveness. My letter was almost cruel. You said you would be more careful in the future, don't. I want you to be careless if you call it carelessness to say what you did. For my sake won't you say that you will <u>never</u> think that I said I loved you <u>because</u> of anything that you ever said. You <u>must</u> say that or I can <u>never be happy.</u>

I would be cruel, yes <u>wicked,</u> to allow whatever you said to cause me to make my confession. Not a bit of it. I love you and I do not know the cause. I suppose there is none. The cause of love is a mystery incomprehensible. I cannot explain it, but let this fact suffice: "<u>I love you.</u>"

As my brother and I were at work today on the back end of the farm away from all civilization, I had a good opportunity to ask him how his life since marriage compared with his life before. He says he doesn't work any harder, and his health is better, and I know that to be true.

I was surprised to find that he knew of our affairs, but I guess all that Emma knows, Hub does. He says he was speaking to Pa about it this morning, and Pa says, "Well, I am going to help him in the fall." He told some one that he was going to town in the fall (I doubt it) and give the farm up to Herb and I. I do not want to do that if I can get on a circuit. Lida isn't any better. We haven't any girl yet. We must have one right away because we are rushed all the time. Well, I guess I had better close my letter for fear I run it into nonsense again.—

Devotedly, Berte—

Yours Affectionately. I hope I shall be received Sunday afternoon with a warm heart and open arms. In my estimation you have <u>not been too hasty.</u> It may be that you have changed your mind. I will know Sunday, I hope.

Yours B.H.I.

◆   ◆   ◆

Thivener, Ohio
June, 1890

Dear Lizzie:--

I would rather have gone down Sun. than to have stayed at home, but you know my reason for staying away from you.

I could come in the day time and not go to Sallie's, but they would kick then sure enough so I guess we will have to suffer for a little while. Only I hope you will be willing to come up here just as soon as you can get ready. I will depend on you to say when you are ready. You said I might make my arrangements, and you would make yours accordingly. (My arrangements are made. All I want is one week's notice. I can get ready now if you say so. But if as you say the work will not slack until Aug. and that will make it a more convenient time, I suppose we must wait until then though it is a long way off. I must not come oftener than two wks. I believe that I can stay away contentedly better by not coming so often.

I am anxious to have you come, but I am afraid to have you come against your will for fear you will be disappointed. I am unworthy, but really I do not feel like giving you up now. I hope that you will be willing to take me with all my bad habits and defects of character. I don't want you unless you have enough confidence in me to believe that I will always be good to you even after your Dear ole Father is gone. You said I would be afraid of him, but of course you were joking. You know that would be no cause for me treating you well. I know for a fact that I will not mistreat you (as long as I keep my senses). If I lose my sense, then I want to be put somewhere where I can't be seen by you or any one else. So of course I can't mistreat you then. So when I mistreat you, you may know by that that I have lost my senses and have me sent off, "done up in small packages". I will be down Sun. unless providence prevents it. We found a girl at last. This is her second wk. More Mon.

Yours, Berte.

◆   ◆   ◆

Thivener, Ohio
June 30, 1890

Dear Celia: E

I believe I will change your name. What do you say?

I am through harvesting wheat and ready for the Hay and Corn. No rest for the weary. It is not because I have so much work to do that I did not come down Sunday. That is not the cause altogether. I find when I do not go so often, I can stay away better than I could if I went every week. I stay close at home now. On Sunday I take Lida and Stella to Sunday School. They impose on me just a little because the Supt. always calls on me to open the Sunday School, and the Class Leader always calls on me to conduct the class meeting. So you see I am having a little exercise now.

I am not yet altogether decided what I will do this fall. Pa said to some one the other day that he was going to move to Gallipolis this fall. If he does, I expect he will want us to live here. I do not want to do that very bad, but you know if we can't do any better, we will take care of the farm for a little while anyway.

Yes, I think your suggestion to get married and go to Camp Meeting is a good one. Thought of that before you mentioned it. Oh, I almost wish I hadn't commenced to write because I am almost sick to see you just now—

Two young ladies have decided that you and I have split and have got badly stuck already. I am very sorry, but I can't help it. The only attention I ever gave to them was to pick up one (Doctor Serrier's girl) and took her home from Sunday School. It was on my way, and she was walking through the boiling sun. I overtook her, and as I had the buggy, I took her as an act of kindness. But it caused her to slight the Dr. for my sake, and now the Dr. is terrible jealous of me. Isn't it funny that smart people are lacking of common sense in some respects.

I do not dare to speak to her any more. It may be better though to be jealous-hearted than not to be jealous at all. I never was enough that way. Such a thing never enters mind. Even if I should catch you with some young man and in the parlor at that, I would believe that it was only a friend unless you would say differently. I never was jealous at all. You need not fear my loyalty and go on with your preparations without fear of my backing out on my part. I suppose you are still in the notion unless you have decided that you are not strong enough. If you are and wish me to know it, do not fear to tell me now. I hope it is not so. If you are strong enough to work every day, why not strong enough to get married. Write to me soon and tell me all the particulars, and I will burn the letter as soon as I read it. I want you to burn this and all the rest right away for fear some one will read some of them. I burned all my letters yesterday except a few from you. That's all I want. Well, I ought to stop writing now and go to work. Hoping that our love for each other will grow stronger. I know it will on my part for you come nearer to my Ideal than any other girl I know or ever expect to know. You come so near my Ideal that I am very sure that I can be happy in your company all the time to the end of time and eternity.

Write soon. Write often. Write a good long letter is the request of your unworthy friend.

Affectionately,

Your Berte.

Excuse paper and scribbling. Don't forget to burn all my letters unless it be a few of the best. Please.

Bye Bye

◆　　　◆　　　◆

Thursday
Thivener, Ohio
July 1890

Dear Lizzie:

I thought of coming down this evening after receiving your letter. So to bring you those cards and see about our affairs, but after giving the affairs a consideration I concluded that it is not absolutely necessary for me to come down before Tuesday Of course you would rather have those cards or envelopes now, but you do not want me to come purposely for that so I will bring them down Tues. and if you do not have time to direct them there, I will or if it doesn't matter, we can send them afterwards.

I have used 12. That is all I can think of now. I have 12 cards and 20 small envelopes not used. I had large envelopes the size of cards so I used them. If you wish to make any change in our arrangements, do so. Just so you make me aware of the fact in time to change my arrangement accordingly. Changing to 1 P.M. is alright just so you make the time shorter. I am not particular about having anyone to stand up with, but really it would take half of the peoples' eyes off of us. Ed says if you want him, he will do his best to stay with us. If it isn't too late, you can tell Duck about it, but I suppose it is too late now. I expect Ed to stump his toe and fall a time or two but that would be no difference to us, if we are lucky enough to get to the altar without falling.

Ed will come down I think. Then you can do as you please about having others. I think Ed wants to come anyway. He says he will do anything that he can for me. The girls bother me so I write some of the words over the second time.

I forgot to say anything about provision. I never thought of it until Ma asked me if I was going to take any, but I will risk going without any. If we get sort of hungry, I will make a Raid on the hospitality of the people at Camp. Ma wanted to know if we were coming direct to our house. I told her I thought we would, but if any change was made we could let know—

I hope you will feel at home here if we should fail to get a circuit. I wouldn't stay at home one minute if you get dissatisfied—

The Doctor has just called and said that he would go down on Wednesday morning, and if we want his services, they are for us, and if we think we can get along without him, it will be alright. So you see my partner is all solid for or against.

You asked me if I regretted taking the step that I have. Why Bless your heart, no! I haven't been idle all the time. I know what I am doing. I have summed you up as being nothing no less than a noble girl, refined and worthy of all the respect and Love that I can give. I am ashamed of some of my actions towards you.

I hope to be better in the future—I do not doubt our happiness or mine at least.

Well, I will see you on Tues. If you want me to know anything about changes etc. you can write to Gallipolis and I will get it Monday or Tuesday.

Bye By

Lovingly,

Yours,

Berte.

◆   ◆   ◆

Celicia Elizabeth Riggs and Berton Hamilton Ingels were wed on August 6, 1890.

◆   ◆   ◆

Thivener, O
Sept 18, 1890

Dear Lizzie,

Brock wouldn't let me have the house. What would be the best: go to town and rent a house and keep Boarders or you come up here? Ma says you can have rooms here. I would have more <u>time</u> here and more <u>satisfaction</u> if I was entirely alone with you. If we can get boarders, I believe we can rent a house, Gilmans House, and live. Would you rather do that? Now I want you to press your real wishes, and then I will comply with them. Write to Gallipolis Monday and tell me just what you would rather I would do.

Jessie seemed to be very well. Bertha says Mama went to Heaven. She wanted to live with Bessie, and if Bessie died, she wanted to live with me. Lida was greatly disappointed because I didn't get the house. She says she won't get well if she has to stay here all winter.

I will write again Monday if I can send it to the office.

Tell me when you can come to see me

Affectionately your

Husband Berte—

◆   ◆   ◆

The last letter in the collection is from Lizzie to Berte. It could be a foreshadowing for the next few years of their marriage.

Raccoon Island, Ohio
Sep 25 1890

My dear Husband:--

I was somewhat disappointed last night because I didn't receive any letter from you saying what we would do. You know I do not like to be expecting bad news; I would rather know the worse and get prepared for it.

Lida is very much disappointed because I won't say you have to go to town. You know I will not say that.

I have been making jellies and canning more fruit so if we should go to housekeeping, we would have some thing to eat. I have enough of such as that so we wouldn't have to buy any.

I put my quilt in the frames yesterday and will soon have it out, but I am ready to go any time you say.

I heard yesterday if we didn't go to housekeeping soon, we wouldn't receive any presents.

I thought sure I would know now what we would do for sure.

I have been about half sick for the past two days. My throat and left lung hurt me so bad. I took cold the other day when was making jelly. I got so warm and cooled off too quick.

Lida came over yesterday to see if I had heard what you are going to do. She said she wouldn't go home if you did. She says she will stay with Aunt Sallie this winter and then go to town in the spring. Some fellow stole one of Jim's horses Monday night and he went Tuesday after it. Found it at Ironton. Had the fellow arrested and brought to Gallipolis last night on the boat. Will have the trial today at nine o'clock.

When will you be down? I made 24 glasses and 2 qt of jellies Tuesday, but not all of it is for us. So you see, I won't starve.

I could draw some of my money if I thought it was necessary for us to live in town, but I know we could make expenses. I will do now just what you have made the decision to do, but we must go by ourselves in the Spring at the very latest.

You will know the reason better than I can tell you now.

Well, I must get to work for I want to get my quilt out in a few days.

Have you been sick?

Aunt Joe is down at Aunt Sallie's making apple butter.

Your loving and devoted

Wife Lizzie

◆   ◆   ◆

0-595-24252-9

CPSIA information can be obtained at www.ICGtesting.com
Printed in the USA
LVOW07s1607140915

454091LV00002B/450/P